Waiting For Unicorns

Waiting
For Unicorns

BETH HAUTALA

SCHOLASTIC INC.

ISBN 978-0-545-92015-5

12 11 10 9 8 7 6 5 4 3 2   16 17 18 19 20/0

Printed in the U.S.A.   40

First Scholastic printing, December 2015

Edited by Liza Kaplan
Design by Siobhán Gallagher
Text set in Baskerville

To my husband, Aaron, and our beautiful children.
Your names are on every wish in my jar.
And they have all been granted.

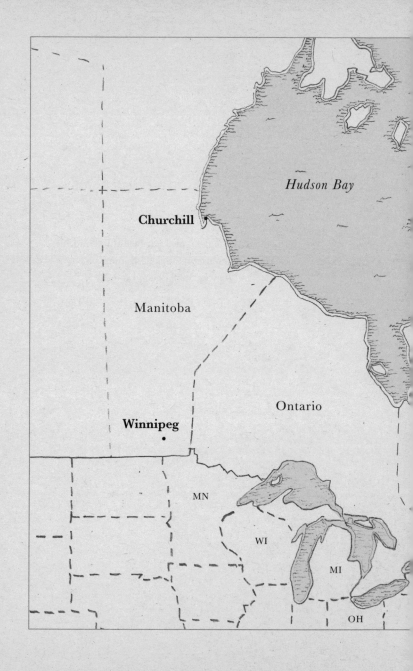

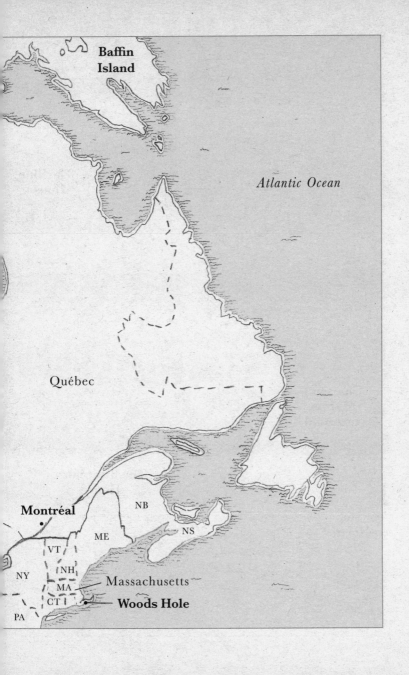

Baffin Island

Atlantic Ocean

Québec

Montréal

NB

ME

NS

VT

NY

NH

MA — Massachusetts

PA

CT — **Woods Hole**

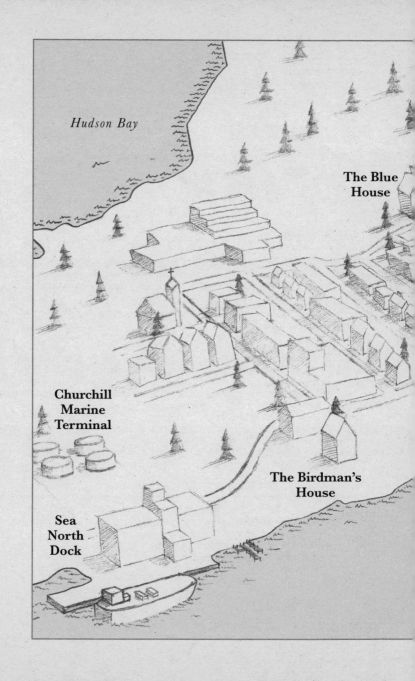

Hudson Bay

The Blue
House

Churchill
Marine
Terminal

The Birdman's
House

Sea
North
Dock

Miss
Piggy

Churchill
Northern
Studies Centre

Churchill River

Prologue

THE INUIT WOMAN TOLD ME that if I ever saw a unicorn, to close my eyes. *Tight*.

"Unicorns break your heart," she said, all the warmth seeping out of her voice. She was warning me against the very thing I was dying to see.

But that's the trouble with things like unicorns. You get hungry for the impossible and it eats at you. Pretty soon, all you can think about is *that thing*—the thing you're supposed to shut your heart to, pretending you never actually cared about it in the first place.

But I did care. And I told myself that when I saw a unicorn, I'd keep my eyes wide, wide open, and just let the sight of it pour into me, breaking up whatever wholeness was left of my heart. And I'd make my wish.

Moving North

IN EARLY MAY, WE MOVED.

It was the first time I'd ever left home for someplace else, and, of course, Dad said it'd be great.

"It'll feel like home in no time," he said.

I didn't believe him, but I didn't tell him that, because it wouldn't have mattered anyway. Home is only home when the people you love live there, and the only person I had left to love was Dad. So I guess home was anywhere he was. Which was fine and easy to say while everyone and everything was familiar. But whether I wanted to go or not, we were leaving the familiar behind. Even the normal end-of-school routine would be different. I'd finish seventh grade far away from the rest of my class and turn in the last of my assignments by mail.

Before we left, Dad and I packed for three days straight.

We taped over the seams of a couple-dozen cardboard boxes, then shipped them away on a cargo plane, and drove north. We were leaving behind our house in Woods Hole, Massachusetts, which was far enough north already in my mind, considering it was only about a five-hour drive to the Canadian line. But one mile-marker at a time, we went right on over the border toward Churchill, Manitoba.

I'd never crossed the border before. It's all very official and serious. The men and women in uniform with stern faces and clipped questions and the Canadian flag flying high over the border station made me nervous. Guilty. Like maybe the stuff we were taking into Canada might be illegal or something. But all I had in my pockets was some Chap-Stick and a candy wrapper. Our duffel bags were just full of clothes, and I guess we must not have looked too suspicious because they didn't ask us to get out of our vehicle for a search or anything.

The border patrol has an interesting job, I think. All the pictures they look at every day—how many driver's licenses and passport pictures do they see?

The photo on my passport wasn't great. I looked too excited about getting my picture taken. My eyes were wide and there was a surprised look on my face. I looked like I thought my whole life was bound to be one big unexpected thing after another. But I don't like change too much, or the unexpected, and it was frustrating that Dad somehow thought all this was a good idea in the first place. Nobody drags their kid to the Arctic for the summer. But my dad was doing just that, and it was surprising how fast my entire life suddenly felt unsteady. Like one big gust of arctic wind could sweep it all away.

Of course, the border patrolman didn't care about any of that. He just asked for my name and matched it to the name printed on my identification. And if he noticed the funny look on my face at all, he probably just thought the lady at the passport office had been quick with her snapshot finger.

"What are you doing in Manitoba?" the patrolman asked.

"Whale research," Dad said. And I was thankful he left it at that, because once he got started talking about whales, there'd be no stopping him.

The patrolman waved us through, and I turned around in my seat, watching as the gate lowered behind us. The border station shrank smaller and smaller as we drove. The road pulled us away from that invisible border line separating the United States from Canada—separating home from everything else. And when I finally turned back around in my seat, it felt like we were going in reverse because I'd been watching the road move away from us for so long. That's what leaving is like. Watching things slip away from you until your insides ache and everything feels backward.

Dad and I drove until we reached Montreal, where a man waited to buy our truck.

"We won't be able to drive past Thompson, Manitoba," Dad said. "No one can, because the roads actually end. And there's no point in having a truck you can't use." He's practical like that.

After Thompson, the roads leading north just stop, giving way to arctic peat bogs and ocean inlets. I'd spent the past few weeks poring over the pictures I'd found online, trying to see it all in my head—something I could barely imagine. I tried to picture the bog lakes and stretches of tamarack trees. In the fall, the trees would trade their green summery clothes for needles the color of saffron—a spice Mom kept in a small glass jar in the spice rack.

But winter was still in charge where we were headed. In the Arctic, things stay cold a whole lot longer than other places. It's too far north to thaw when farther south everything is getting on with the business of spring.

The Montreal man who bought our truck seemed nice enough, though I don't remember very much about him. The only thing that really stuck in my mind was his hair. It sprouted wildly out of his head, and once in a while he ran a hand through it, trying to calm it down. But it wouldn't be calmed and kept falling into his face, where it got mixed up in his eyebrows. There was even hair coming out of his ears and poking up through his dirty flannel shirt where he'd left it unbuttoned, and though I tried to ignore it, out of his nose, too.

I didn't think I'd care who bought our truck. But when it came right down to it, I did. I guess I'd envisioned people like us having the Ford, and somehow, I couldn't make this man and whatever family he might have fit that picture. It made saying good-bye to the old green truck even harder than I thought it'd be. Strange, how you can get attached to something that's done nothing but carry you from one place to the next.

The Ford had carried me to school on snowy days when Mom and Dad didn't trust the buses.

It had carried us to Dairy Queen on hot summer nights. Dad would let me ride in the back, just as long as I sat down and leaned against the cab. He would take the back roads and roll the windows down so that his country music could pour out into the summer air. Mom would sing along, letting the wind carry her voice. She always opened the back window so I could sing along, too, and she held my hand through the space there, like she was afraid I'd blow away in all that warm summer wind.

And of course, the Ford took us to the hospital and back, over and over again, when Mom got sick.

But we left the Ford behind, along with all those memories, and boarded a plane that would bring us closer to Dad's whales. We would have to take two of them: a big plane from

Montreal to Winnipeg, and a smaller one from Winnipeg to Churchill.

And as our plane bounced once before lurching into Canadian skies, I wondered what would be carrying me around next.

Churchill

WHEN HE WASN'T OUT ON expedition, Dad taught at Woods Hole Oceanographic Institution, which meant that sometimes he had a normal everyday job like other dads, and sometimes he didn't.

This summer the marine biology department had offered Dad a fantastic opportunity—they were sending him and a small team of researchers into the arctic waters of Hudson Bay and the Baffin Island inlets to do whale research for three months.

But it wasn't the first time Dad had been to Churchill to study the whales. He'd actually been there a bunch of times. In fact, this is where he started his whale research, way back when he was an undergraduate at the institution. So Dad knew people in Churchill. He had friends here—people he'd known for a long time. And he had a place to do his work. The Churchill Northern Studies Centre, or the CNSC, would serve as home base for Dad and his team while they did their research. But I'd never been here before and everything was strange. There were no familiar faces for me and no familiar names. Nothing but the unknown.

Even though Dad had been to Churchill on plenty of expeditions in the past, this was the first time the institution had ever offered to fund one of his expeditions. And it was the first time I'd ever come along. Sometimes, Mom and I had gone to visit Dad while he was away on trips like this one, though never to Churchill. And those trips had always been a kind of short vacation for us. We'd never stayed for an entire summer.

When Dad told me about our summer plans he said they were only temporary. And I know he was trying to make me feel better. But it didn't work, because all I could think about was how the permanent things were slipping away. Just this year, I'd said good-bye to all my friends, and my home, now our green truck, and Mom. Even though we were only leaving for three months, I couldn't help but feel like the only things left were temporary.

Churchill, Manitoba, sits all huddled up on the shores of Hudson Bay, where ice and snow try to keep it in deep freeze. But the boreal forest—old and green with lichen, black spruce, highbush cranberries, and the tundra—strewn with glacial rock as old as the earth itself, makes the place more than just a tiny arctic community on the edge of the great cold.

"It's a beautiful place, Tal," Dad said over the whine of the airplane's engine. "People come from all over to visit because it's magic, you know." He winked at me. I rolled my eyes and looked out the window.

I couldn't see much down there, just a shift in colors as we went farther and farther north. At first there was only green, the soft new kind—new leaves and springtime spread out below me. All the trees at home had thrown on their springtime dresses weeks ago, but these trees wore the fresh green of brand new leaves. As we kept going, the forest underneath us got darker and richer. Dad told me the names of those dark green trees as we flew over—evergreens. "They will never lose their leaves as the seasons change," he said. "That's how they got their name. But there's also spruce, cedar, red and white pine, and redwoods down there, too." He was so in awe of this place. I just nodded.

After that the landscape changed even more dramatically—the old green shifted to white until there was only a blanket of snow beneath us, stretching out in all directions. And that's all I'd see until we landed in Churchill. People who come here for fun must be crazy. Why would anyone want to go someplace so far away from absolutely everything? So cold, and white, and *winter*?

I knew why people came to Churchill, of course. They came for arctic adventure. They came to see the polar bears and the rare arctic birds. Mostly, they came for the whales. I knew this because that's what Churchill's official website said, under the "Things To Do" section. I never would have come for these things, but I didn't have a choice in the matter. Even if I did, Dad and I wouldn't be doing any wildlife tours together. I'd be stuck in town while he was out on the ice, because even though I was here for my dad, he was here for the whales. You could have tossed out every other interesting thing about Churchill, and he'd still come. That's how much those whales mattered to Dad. Lucky for him, Churchill is the self-proclaimed "Beluga Capital of the World."

To the south of town, the Churchill River runs wide-mouthed into Hudson Bay. And it's there, at the mouth of the river, where thousands of little white whales come up out of the Arctic Sea. The water is warmer where it empties into the bay, and June through August, belugas come here to feed, give birth, raise their babies, and catch up with each other. By late August there can be more than three thousand belugas in the Churchill River estuary.

Dad's heart belonged to the whales. It always had. Mom told me she knew this when she married him.

"I'd rather he be out there, doing what he loves, even if it means being away from us and missing us, than if he did something he hates closer to home. Wouldn't you?"

"But it's lonely without him," I protested, and she agreed.

"I wish he was closer, too. But we all do the best we can. And he'll always come back to us, Tal. You can count on that. He will leave those whales of his—let them go off without him, and hurry home to us because we're his family."

Mom had been certain family meant more to Dad than anything else. I wonder what she would think if she could see us now.

Dad and I sat crammed together in our uncomfortable airplane seats trying not to crowd one another, which was pretty much impossible. There was only one armrest between us and I didn't know if it was his or mine. He didn't seem to know either, so we both just avoided it. An armrest-shaped wall between us.

"People used to believe whales were magic, too," Dad said.

I waited for him to continue, to explain which whales, and why people thought they were magic, but he never did. Dad did that a lot—started a thought and forgot to finish it. I think he forgot I was there, listening, waiting for him.

Mom never did that. She always finished her thoughts, always finished her stories. She collected them, studying languages, people groups, and the tales that, she said, tie us all together. And when she got down to the business of telling a new story, you might as well just drop everything. She wouldn't stop till it was over, and you wouldn't be able to focus on much else until she did anyway.

She always started exactly the same way.

"I've got a new one for you, Tal," she'd say. And she'd pause, long and hard. When I was little, I used to think she paused like this because she was making things up in her head as she went, or because she wanted to be certain I was paying attention. Now I know she paused because she was feeling the story's weight.

"A story never belongs to just one person," she explained to me. "It belongs to every person who has ever told it, and to every person who has ever heard it. And that makes storytelling quite an important thing."

But as I stared out the plane's window watching the topsides of clouds floating past, I shook off thoughts of Mom. Sometimes it just hurt too much to remember.

We arrived in Churchill on May fifteenth. I watched Dad mark off the day in his little green pocket calendar before tucking it back in the front pocket of his shirt and patting it reassuringly. Dad has carried a pocket calendar with him for as long as I can remember, marking off the days as we lived them.

He said it was easier to carry all of your days when you've got them with you. But I wondered if he kept his little calendar because it made him feel like he was big enough to go on without Mom. Did he mark the days since she'd been gone, like I did?

Our first night in Churchill, when the arctic wind beat against our motel, and the sound of my dad snoring came clear across the hall, I felt the weight of our days myself. My chest ached from the strain of a million held-back tears, but I fought to keep them in. And in the early spring darkness, when the purple and green aurora borealis washed against the arctic sky and the still, frozen surface of Hudson Bay, I remembered Mom's stories.

Polar Bear, Polar Bear

I WAS IN CHURCHILL FOR three whole days before I saw a bear. I was kind of surprised it took so long because besides whales, Churchill is famous for polar bears, and I am terrified of them.

Despite what you might think, they're not cute, or friendly, or wary of people. They're just hungry. You might as well be wearing an "Eat Me, I'm Tasty" sign.

Manitoba Conservation even employs a bear patrol year-round to help keep the bears out of town—all twelve hundred of them. And Churchill is a pretty small town. Less than a thousand people live there. So, if you were going to be picky about the math, there were enough bears for every person to have one. And some people could have two.

The bears are always there, but they don't wander into

Churchill very much until bear season begins in October, when they come in off the tundra and wait at the edge of Hudson Bay for ice to form. Then they head out on the floes to hunt seals. I knew this because that's what Churchill's official website said about the matter, and I'd read as much as I could. Just to be certain I was prepared. Being prepared is sort of important, if you think about it. The more prepared you are for things, the less chance they have of surprising you. Or scaring you. Or breaking your heart.

But no amount of preparation could have helped me feel ready for the actual sight of a real, live *nanuq*. Dad and I were on our way to the airport to pick up our boxes, snug in an old Suburban we'd found to handle the icy roads and snow, when a big white polar bear strolled lazily across the road, pausing to study us. Dad slowed down to a full stop. I tightened my fingers around the edges of my seat as my heart started jumping around in my chest.

"Tal, look at her! She's beautiful. *Beautiful!*"

Tall and almost lanky, she seemed cool and indifferent. She might as well have owned that road. Her face was long and narrow, and her eyes seemed very dark and tiny against all that white fur. She was impressive and *terrible*, that's what she was. But Dad would have been disappointed if I didn't look excited.

"Uh-huh. Beautiful," I said, chewing on the ends of my hair.

Until then, the closest I'd ever been to a polar bear was at the zoo in Massachusetts. I'd watched an old bear named Bjorn swim around his glass-walled enclosure, and I'd pressed my hands to the glass, measuring their size against the bear's paws, surprised to find myself so small.

As I sat beside Dad, and as that big white bear examined me from the other side of the windshield, I felt that same smallness and fear creep back in. I tried to ignore what I'd learned—that a polar bear can run up to twenty-five miles per hour—fast enough to catch our Suburban before we could really pick up any speed. Not that it would actually chase us down the road or anything. Still, Dad's reassuring hand on my shoulder was nice, and the rifle stashed under the seat made me a tiny bit braver. That gun was one of the first things Dad had picked up once we arrived in Churchill, along with the Suburban. Even before we got groceries or anything. It was for emergencies. We were prepared.

Our cardboard boxes were waiting for us, neatly stacked in the airport's cargo terminal, and a bittersweet, homesick feeling rolled around in the pit of my stomach at the sight of them. Our handwriting was familiar, reminding me of their contents. But the boxes seemed out of place, as if they'd time-traveled—small, square packages full of home, way out here on the edge of the Arctic.

Dad and I were quiet as we drove away from the airport.

He must have been thinking about Mom, because at one point he reached over and tugged on my ear, like she used to do. It bugged me.

"I'm all right you know," I said, leaning my head back against the seat, out of his reach. He just nodded.

Sometimes I thought I could fool him—thought I could pretend hard enough to convince both of us. Over the last few months, we'd grown so busy trying to convince each other that we were all right—that we were doing okay without her—that now there was this space the exact size of Mom standing between us. And no amount of pretending could fill it.

There'd always been a kind of space between Dad and me, maybe because he was away so much. But now that Mom was gone, that space seemed like a dangerous thing. What if it got bigger? Losing Mom was bad enough. I didn't want to lose my dad, too. I wasn't even sure if he felt that space. Maybe it only existed from my side and he couldn't feel it. Or maybe it was all in my head, like that warning on the side-view mirrors of a car: "Objects in mirror are closer than they appear." But that space certainly felt real, and I didn't know how to close it up. Especially now that we'd be apart for most of the summer.

We were renting two rooms in a house right on the edge of town. Dad had stayed there before. He was friends with the Inuit woman who lived there. And while it was nice of her to welcome my dad and me into her house, I wasn't exactly excited about spending my summer with a stranger while Dad was out on the ice.

"I've been friends with Sura for a long time, Tal," Dad said. "Your mom, too. We came to Churchill together a couple of times before you were born," he said. "She and Sura knew each other. She never told you?"

I shook my head. Mom had told me things about Churchill, but she never told me she'd been here herself. I just figured she knew things because of what Dad had told her, same as me. It was a new thought. My mom had been here, sat beside my dad as they drove along these roads. She'd seen these same trees and glacial rocks, the same sweep of the shore, ice-locked and covered in snow.

I held that thought, clung to it as we pulled up next to the house, the back of the Suburban loaded with our boxes. Instead of clapboard siding, the house was covered with blue asphalt shingles from peak to porch. The whole structure seemed to sag a bit, as if it were leaning into the wind whipping shoreward off the frozen surface of Hudson Bay.

"So what do you think?" Dad asked, reaching over and patting my knee.

"It looks good," I said, and I scrunched up my mouth into what I hoped looked like a smile.

He studied my face for a minute and sighed. Then he nodded once like he'd made up his mind, and got out. The cold air whooshed into the warm cab as he slammed the door behind him.

The engine ticked quietly, cooling in the arctic air. My breath fogged up the windows, making everything seem calm and far away through the cloudy glass. I sat in the car, waiting for just the right moment, taking in the sight of the place that would be my home for the next few months. I wasn't ready to jump right into this new life just yet. So I took that pause. The same one Mom used to take before she began a story. Then I took a deep breath and opened the door. It screeched wide on frozen hinges.

The wind whipped around me, stinging my face and bare hands. I dug into my pockets for my mittens and tucked my chin into my coat collar. Anything to protect myself from the cold.

Dad didn't seem to mind it, though. He was waiting, one hand stuffed deep into his pocket, the other ready to land on my shoulder. I dodged his arm, and we walked to the front steps with a Mom-sized space between us.

A dark-haired woman in a yellow sweater stood on the porch. She was a splash of color in that cold, drab world, like that jar of saffron in the pantry.

"Welcome back, Thomas," she said to my dad, taking his hand in both of hers. I stood behind him on the steps, one hand pressed against the railing to steady myself.

Her voice was surprising. Deep and rich and smooth as

chocolate. She was nothing like what I'd expected. She was quite pretty. Her skin was darker than mine, and her eyes were smaller. Her hair was black and shiny and fell thick just past her shoulders. And she was younger than I thought she'd be, not much older than my mom, actually. In my head she'd been old and gray haired, her skin wrinkled like the paper we'd packed around our belongings from home. All of a sudden I had to rearrange some of the things I'd been imagining about her.

"Sura, this is my daughter, Talia Lea McQuinn," Dad said, gesturing awkwardly as I joined them on the porch. She knew who I was, of course, just like I knew her. Dad had spent the last several weeks talking about her, where she lived, how her culture was different than ours. He was preparing me, I suppose.

I did my best to return Sura's warm smile, but the cold had seeped into me, slowing everything down, and I couldn't seem to get my lips to move much. I leaned against the house, comforted by the shingle siding, rough as sandpaper under my palm.

"Blue, like the bay in August when the ice is out," Sura said, nodding at the siding.

She could have told me how good it was to finally meet me, how much she hoped Churchill would feel like home, or what great friends she knew we were going to be. But she didn't. Maybe Sura knew better than to pretend. She traced the edge of a blue shingle with her fingers and then glanced out over the snow and ice to where the vast expanse of Hudson Bay finally met the horizon.

I could live here, if I had to, in this house that leaned into the arctic wind. It wasn't home, but it was certainly better than the hotel where Dad and I had been staying for the last three days while we waited for our things to arrive.

"Welcome to Churchill, Talia Lea," Sura said finally. Her words gently broke the silence that had crept into all of us, standing out there on her porch.

Her English was smooth, though I could tell she used a different language more often than the one I was familiar with.

"It's just Talia," I said. Her gaze and unexpected warmth made my face feel hot.

She nodded and held the door wide, leading Dad and me inside.

Moraine

THE BLUE HOUSE WAS TALL and skinny with two bedrooms on top and two bedrooms below. The bathroom, kitchen, and main living spaces were all squeezed onto the main floor. Dad and I would sleep upstairs, and Sura downstairs, leaving one room empty. She would rent this out to tourists later in the season.

My bedroom was exactly the same as Dad's—small with low ceilings. Dad could only stand upright in the middle of the room, where the ceiling rose up to the peak of the house, otherwise he bumped his head. It was easier for me because I was smaller, but I still had to watch my head around the window alcove.

The blue house sat on the edge of town, and when I craned my neck just right, I could see Hudson Bay from my bedroom window. It was frozen solid, which is how it would stay until July, and I tried not to be too discouraged about that.

"By July things will warm just enough to break up the ice," Dad said, his voice echoing in my small, empty room. "And it will begin to form all over again just a few months later."

He wanted me to be as amazed as he was. It *was* pretty amazing that a place could spend so much time frozen solid and still live. But all I could think about was how cold it was, and how cold it was going to stay. I don't like having to pull on layers of socks and sweater after sweater until my body feels thick and I can't bend my elbows very well. Even in mid-summer, temperatures in Churchill hang right around sixty-two degrees. I wouldn't need my bathing suit.

Breathing on the window, I made a small patch of fog and wrote my name on the glass with my finger. Then I drew a sad face. Dad cleared his throat and I turned around, kept my gaze on the small bed frame and mattress, the dresser, and the empty bookcase before meeting his eyes. My dad stood with his hair brushing against the ceiling. A giant man in a tiny room full of echoes.

"Whad'ya say we bring up our stuff?" he asked, motioning toward the door. I followed him downstairs and out into the cold.

Until Mom got sick, I never really had to think about how much stuff I owned. I had tons of collections; Mom called me a pack rat.

"Look at all of this junk, Talia!" she said one afternoon. I was supposed to be cleaning my room, but I'd gotten distracted.

"It's not junk!" I said. "These things are important!"

"Well, if you don't get all of your important things picked up before dinner, I'll take care of them myself."

"You mean throw them away."

She folded her arms across her chest, which was all the answer I needed. Mom was generally pretty understanding when it came to my collections. She had some herself, but when things started sprawling over into places they didn't belong, she got rid of them.

"Tal, you don't even need these things." She picked up an old plastic Easter egg full of Scrabble tiles, and a broken compass. "Why are you saving these?"

"Those are from the time I got bingo." I nodded at the Scrabble tiles. "They're lucky! I played every tile on one turn."

She rolled them around in the palm of her hand. "And what was the word?"

"Moraine."

"Moraine?"

"Yeah. The stuff that's left behind when a glacier melts."

She sighed, then dropped the tiles into my hand, like my answer had just given them meaning. "And the compass?"

I shrugged. "It used to point north."

"But Tal, it's broken. The needle just spins."

"I know. But it used to work. And that counts for something, right?" She shook her head like she thought I was a little crazy and handed me the compass. Sometimes she just didn't understand.

After Mom died, Dad and I moved out of our house to a smaller apartment. There just wasn't enough room to take everything with me, so I'd thrown a lot of my stuff away. I didn't need it. It was just clutter, really. Things that reminded me of other things. And some of them I didn't want to remember anymore. But I saved the Scrabble tiles and the compass.

At the time, I remember being surprised by how easily my entire life fit into boxes, and now, as Dad unloaded one carton of our lives after another, that same feeling washed over me again. Our entire life had been reduced to a load small enough for one man to carry.

My name was written across my boxes in permanent marker, and I picked one up, being careful to knock the snow from my boots before carrying it into the house. It felt nice, having my own familiar things back.

Sura held the door for us as we traipsed in and out, making small talk with Dad. I knew she knew about Mom, though she never actually said anything. You can always tell when people are trying not to talk about something. Their voices are too bright and don't match their words. But I'm glad she didn't ask us how we were. People asked that all the time, expecting it to be an easy question to answer, but I never knew what to say, so I usually just kept quiet.

While Dad and Sura chatted, I climbed up and down the stairs in this strange new place, each box held tight against my chest. When I had carried everything up to my room, I began peeling back the tape and opening them up.

Clothes and blankets came first, followed by shoes and the red wool hat my neighbor had made for me. I pulled that hat on and tugged it down over my ears before digging back into the rest of the boxes.

Books and photographs were next. There were photographs of school friends, of Dad and me at the state fair, him, me, and Mom standing in front of our old house. And there was one of Mom looking over her shoulder, laughing as she walked away from the camera. I picked up that picture, studying it.

Everyone said I looked like her. I had her same wide-set eyes and turned-up nose, and I liked that. Our hair was the same, too—long and brown and straight. When I was little, I wore it short—bobbed at my chin. But it was long now, partly because Mom was the one who used to trim it for me, and partly because I wanted to look like her as much as I could. I wanted to hold onto her every time I looked in the mirror. But sometimes, when I saw my mom's face looking back at me, I wondered what else we shared. Would I get her cancer, too?

After I unpacked the photographs, I opened a box of random stuff I hadn't wanted to leave behind. There was a valentine from a boy at my old school, a pencil holder I'd made out of Popsicle sticks, old diaries, and a few stuffed animals.

I put my things away, stacking books on the wobbly bookcase, hanging my clothes neatly in the closet, lining my shoes along the floor, and spreading my quilt from home across the bed.

Lastly, I unwrapped a sheet of crumpled packing paper from around a large glass mason jar half full of little paper slips. It didn't look that impressive, but this jar—these slips of paper—were the most important things I owned. My wishes.

I held the jar up to the window. The light seemed to collect inside the glass, illuminating each paper slip. I shook the jar, shifting the slips around, rearranging them, settling them. I wouldn't take them out tonight. I'd let them adjust to our new room first.

I pushed the jar under my bed and leaned back against the bed frame, checking my work.

"Better," I whispered.

It was less full of echoes, but it wasn't home and I knew it never would be. I just had to get through the next few months. Then Dad and I could go back to Woods Hole and I could forget this place and finally start over.

Full of Snowflakes

I WOKE THE FIRST MORNING in the blue house and lay very still in my bed, staring up at the ceiling. It was dark, but the light from the hall spilled under the crack in my bedroom door. The old cast-iron radiator in the corner of my room clunked and gurgled. It had made those noises all night long. Sura warned me it would, but it still sounded strange. We'd had central heat in our apartment back home, and the baseboards would tick as they warmed up, but they were polite about it. This old thing was downright ridiculous. I glared at the radiator as it clunked and gurgled again.

The smell of coffee climbed the stairs, and Dad's bedroom door across the hall creaked open on rusty hinges. His footfalls were quiet, but the floorboards still squeaked under his weight as he made his way down the stairs. I heard his muted voice greet Sura, and her muffled response.

I lay there for a minute, listening to them talk before sighing and throwing back my covers to search for a sweatshirt and a thick pair of socks. I didn't want to stay up here in bed while they talked about me down there. I didn't need Dad telling Sura any personal stuff when I wasn't there to defend myself. She didn't need to know a single thing about me that I wasn't willing to share on my own.

The stairs squeaked as I padded downstairs, a pair of Dad's wool socks on my feet. I tucked my hair behind my ears and both Sura and Dad looked up from their places in the kitchen. He was at the table with his big hands around a steaming cup of coffee, and Sura was flipping pancakes at the stove.

"Morning, Tal, how'd ya sleep?" Dad's grin was wide and hopeful. He wanted this to be all right. He wanted me to be okay.

"Fine," I said.

"Do you like pancakes, Talia?" Sura held out her spatula, a perfect golden cake balancing on the end of it.

I shrugged. "They're okay."

Dad threw me a look, but I ignored it and sat down across the table.

I loved pancakes and Dad knew it. Actually, I loved my *mom's* pancakes. She made them from scratch with oat flour. They tasted like oatmeal and pancakes all rolled into one. Breakfast perfection.

"Well, your dad said you were a fan." Sura was unfazed,

and she placed a plate of pancakes in front of me. "If you don't like them I have *tuktu* and *touton*," she said.

Dad laughed, and I glanced up at her.

"What is that?"

"Caribou and bread fried in bear fat," Dad said.

I quickly stuffed a bite of pancake in my mouth.

Strange places and strange people were one thing, but strange food was another. I smiled, a tiny bit nervous as Sura handed me a glass of orange juice. What sort of people ate caribou? And then there was *whale*! Dad told me whale meat was a regular delicacy around here.

"These are great," I said between bites. I pushed the pancakes around my plate.

"I'm going to head on over to the CNSC this morning and start mapping out the expedition details," Dad said to me. "Want to come along?"

I wanted to go with him. There was an empty loneliness in me, yawning wide. It had been open ever since Mom died, but it was opening up even more now that Dad was so close to leaving. Normally I would have jumped at the chance to join him. And I should have jumped now; it might have gone a little way in closing up that Mom-sized space. But I shook my head. Something kept me from saying yes.

Dad had planned this trip a while ago. Before we knew how serious things were with Mom. And when she died, he should have called it off. He should have stayed home. He should have let *me* stay home. What would Mom think right now, if she knew? If she knew he'd gone on with his work and life and stuff just like nothing had changed. What would she say if she knew he had dragged me out here with him for the summer, only to leave me with someone I didn't even know?

But Mom wasn't here.

What was I supposed do once Dad disappeared out on the ice? Hanging over his shoulder at the CNSC while he got ready to leave me wasn't going to help. The emptiness inside me was loud and insistent. I needed to be alone while I figured out what to do with it.

"Think I'll just stay here," I said. "I want to look around."

Dad looked surprised, and then sort of relieved. And I suddenly felt horrible. Mad even. I didn't actually want to do anything of the sort. What I really wanted was to go back upstairs to my room and hide under the covers until spring came to this icy, frozen-over place. But it was easier to lie than tell him we'd both better get used to being alone. And Dad didn't seem too concerned anyway.

"Well, you have fun exploring," Dad said as he got up to leave. "Just make sure you let Sura know where you're headed."

I nodded and watched him walk down the hall as he pulled his parka from its hook on the wall. Until he left, Dad would spend the next week or so inland, preparing his team for the first of several expeditions out on the ice. They'd head north out over the floes and explore the eastern edge of Hudson Bay and the Foxe Basin for beluga activity.

And I knew I'd be safe here while he was away. Safer than if I was out on the ice, anyway. I could even go exploring around town if I wanted. Dad didn't want me getting lost, but there wasn't much chance of that considering I had no intention of actually leaving the house. Or my room for that matter.

"See you later tonight," Dad called over his shoulder. But I just stared down at the brown pool of maple syrup on my plate, blinking as the front door slammed behind him.

The kitchen was very quiet for a few minutes, and then Sura pulled out a chair and sat down beside me. She spun her coffee cup in a slow circle while I tried to think of something to say.

"I'm glad you're here, Talia," she began. "I know this must all seem very different from what you're used to. And I'm sure it's going to be awkward at first, being here."

Awkward was putting it mildly. How normal was it to spend a summer in the Arctic with someone you've never met?

I squirmed in my chair. Sura didn't avoid the obvious like Dad and I were so used to doing. It made me uncomfortable, like I'd forgotten to put on clothes before coming downstairs.

Whether Sura could tell I was uncomfortable or not

she didn't show it. She just kept trying to make me feel at home.

"It's a good thing for Churchill—you and your father being here," she said. "We depend on the whales to draw in tourists, so we need the whale watchers, the photographers, and the naturalists to continue visiting. They keep our little town on the map. Your dad's research will help to ensure our whales keep coming back, year after year." Environmental and climate changes could potentially alter their route, but I knew from science class that even if they stray off course, whales return to the same places to eat and rest every year. As long as conditions remain favorable, they will hunt in the same places, too, and follow the same ocean currents, which makes it possible for researchers, like my dad, to study them.

I'd also learned that whales are repetitive creatures. Dad said they're like stubborn old men. *Once they get set in their ways, they settle down and stay put.* That's why Churchill was so important. This was home to those whales. Nothing on earth would make them fail to return.

Sura looked up at me over the rim of her coffee cup, her eyes warm. I twisted my napkin into tiny little pieces until it looked like my lap was full of snowflakes.

I should have been glad to be here. To be away from everything that reminded me of Mom. And I should've been happy my dad was making a difference. But the small selfish part of me kept creeping in and twisting my sadness into anger. I wanted my dad to myself. I didn't want to share him with Churchill or with Churchill's little white whales. And I didn't want Sura to be glad about us being here. I wanted her to feel upset with my dad for dragging me out here and then leaving, like I was.

"Thanks for the pancakes," I said.

I gathered up the bits of napkin in my lap and looked around the kitchen for a trash can. I didn't want to sit here anymore. I didn't want Sura to know how hard I was fighting the lump in my throat.

"The garbage is under the sink," she said. "Or I can take that for you."

I shook my head and jumped up, my fist clenched around my twisted, shredded napkin.

"I got it," I said, dropping the pieces into the trash can.

I muttered an excuse about unpacking some more of my things and hurried up the stairs to my room, my sadness twisting inside until my heart felt small and cold and in pieces. Just like snowflakes.

Missing

DAD AND HIS TEAM SPENT the next week and a half getting ready for their first short-term expedition, and I pretended like I wasn't counting every hour, every minute until he left me. I finished all of my end-of-the-year school assignments, reread two of the books I'd brought from home, and spent a lot of time just standing at my bedroom window, staring out over the frozen landscape. It was the third week in May, but there was still snow on the ground, and it was below freezing. Spring didn't seem like much of a possibility way out here.

I knew what snow looked like, obviously, but I wasn't used to the colorful whiteness of everything—the different shades and textures. Like the clouds that scuttled across the sky, trying to outrun the north wind, the snow was full of colors. If I were a painter I'd have to use grays and browns, blues, pinks, and yellows in addition to whites to get it right. And that was on a cloudy day. But when the sun broke, there was no hope of ever getting that snow right, no matter how many colors you might have in your palette.

I've heard people say freshly fallen snow is blinding. But I never really understood what that meant until now. When the sun hit the frozen bay, the new snow looked like it was lit from underneath. It was almost as if the sun had somehow broken itself apart and burrowed under the arctic landscape until all of its warmth seeped out, leaving behind only its cold brilliant light.

I also watched people come and go. Since Sura's house was on the edge of town, it was pretty much just hunters and trappers venturing out past the house into the tundra. With their snowmobiles whining and spewing exhaust into the cold air, they would drag their gear behind them in sleds, cutting a wide swath through the snow. It was a strange sight, watching them disappear into the frozen landscape, a rifle strapped to their backs. Sura said they were hunting tuktu—caribou, mostly. Sometimes moose.

"Most of what we eat comes from the land," she said. "Or off the ice."

"Aren't there laws against hunting in the springtime?" I asked.

Sura smiled. "There are. Though I'm surprised you know about that."

"Why are you surprised?" I glanced up at her and crossed my arms. My dad had been a whale researcher my whole life. Was it really so shocking that I would know some stuff about animal rights?

"I just didn't realize you thought about hunting regulations," Sura said carefully, "especially in regards to your dinner."

I didn't really know how to respond to that. I hadn't talked to Sura much since we'd arrived, so this—being around her—was all still pretty new. Instead I just asked again, "So is he hunting illegally?"

"No. Standard hunting regulations do not apply to the Inuit because we depend on the animals in ways other people do not. We do not take them for sport, but for survival. There is a difference."

I nodded. "Tuktu." I said the word for caribou in Sura's native language clumsily, feeling its heaviness against my tongue.

"Yes. The life of a caribou for the life of the Inuit. And you."

I wanted to tell Sura I hoped they weren't out there killing caribou for my sake, but I didn't say anything.

By May twenty-fourth, Dad was ready to leave for his first expedition. The morning of his departure, I stuck pretty close to him, partly because I didn't want to lose sight of him before I had to, and partly because I didn't want to keep running into Sura. The house was pretty small, and it seemed that no matter where I went she was lurking just around the corner, waiting to see if we needed anything. I couldn't exactly tell her that what I needed was to be at home—to have my mom back—to be anywhere but here in the middle of Churchill, Manitoba, because if I was here, that meant my dad was still leaving and my mom was still gone. And there wasn't much Sura could do to change that.

While Dad packed, I sat cross-legged on his bed, running my palms over the patchwork quilt that covered it. I watched as he filled his duffel bag—wool socks, sweaters, long underwear, sun goggles, sunscreen. I tried to pretend he was just leaving for the weekend.

"Maybe you'll get a nice tan," I said jokingly. But I knew better, and so did Dad. In fact, the sun was so strong out on the ice that in addition to needing sunscreen to protect his skin, Dad needed to protect his eyes, too. Like sunburn on your eyes, the glare off the brilliant snow stretching out for endless miles in all directions could shut you up in darkness if you weren't careful. Snow blindness was a real thing—temporary, but painful. The Inuit had known all about this for ages, and long before we came along, they were wearing snow goggles carved from whale bone with slits to see through.

But snow blindness was the least of Dad's concerns.

Ever since we'd come to town, we'd been hearing reports from hunters and trappers as they came in off the ice. Dad said it was the strangest thing he'd ever heard, and I could tell he didn't quite believe it.

There were no whales. That's what they were saying.

"What if you can't find them?" I asked.

Dad shrugged and grinned. "It's early. Sometimes currents and water temperatures shift just enough to alter migration patterns a little. Nothing to worry about. I'll only be gone for a few days," he promised. "I'll just take some measurements and water samples, and then I'll be back."

And with that, he left me at the blue house with Sura.

When Dad radioed just two days later to tell us he was coming in off the ice, I could tell by the sound of his voice that something was wrong.

The night Dad came home, Sura cooked a huge dinner to celebrate his return. She went all out. Maybe she hoped that surprising him with his favorite meal would cheer him up. But Sura's efforts fell flat because Dad was so wrapped up in his whales—or rather, the *lack* of them.

He and his team had run a variety of tests sampling ice and water, testing salinity and current shifts. They'd done sonar scans, and dropped giant booms through the ice into the depths of Hudson Bay, listening for whale song. But the sea was quiet.

I couldn't help but think maybe something terrible had happened to them. Dad had told me that beluga whales stay near the edge of the ice pack where holes in the ice allow them to surface and breathe. But if it suddenly gets very cold and those holes freeze over, or if the ice shifts, cutting off their route to open water, the pod can become trapped. If the whales can't break through the newly formed ice, or if open water is beyond the distance they can swim without surfacing, they can drown. Whales are mammals, and they have to breathe air, just like people. They can hold their breath for a long time, longer than humans, but even the best breath-holders in the world have to come up for air eventually.

"It doesn't make sense, Tal," Dad said to me, stabbing his fork through noodles, sauce, and ricotta cheese. "They've never been this late to Churchill."

"You think something happened to them?" I picked at the crunchy edges of my bread.

"I don't know. Even below-average temperatures wouldn't strand an entire migratory population," Dad said, his voice sharp with frustration. "Something is holding them up. I can't figure it out."

He got up from the table and dropped his plate in the sink. It only took him a few minutes to throw on a coat and boots before he clomped back out the door into the arctic night air, the door slamming behind him. I heard the Suburban sputter to life, protesting the cold, and then he was gone again—back to the CNSC to try and make sense of it all.

I spun my spoon around and around on the smooth surface of the table, watching it catch the light from the low-hanging lamp over my head.

Dad needed those whales—he needed them like I needed Mom's stories, because sometimes you just need something bigger than yourself to feel whole. To keep all the pieces of yourself from falling apart. Those whales were big enough to keep Dad together, but not if he couldn't find them.

And then what?

We were already pretty broken, Dad and I. We couldn't handle too many more missing pieces.

Jar of Wishes

WITH DAD'S RECEDING footsteps and the slam of the front door still resounding in my head, I stretched out on my bedroom floor, my knees and elbows digging into the wide-plank floorboards. My fingers met the cool solidness of my jar of wishes beneath the bed, and I pulled it from the dark into the light of my room. My wishes had settled nicely.

I don't think Dad knew about my wishes, or if he did, he never said. Probably because he wouldn't have known what to do with them.

The first wish I'd ever written was easy to pick out, even though the jar was full of little paper slips. It was more crumpled than the others and the ink was smeared a bit where I'd cried on it. Even the paper looked different. Less white. Older. I'd almost thrown that wish away, because it was so obviously not coming true. But I kept it, in the end.

Mom had fingered it like the petals of a flower when I showed it to her.

I wish there was no more cancer.

Then she'd kissed it and dropped it into my jar herself. I couldn't throw it away after that because it wasn't just my wish. Mom and I had both wished for her cancer to go away.

Over the next few months, she added two more wishes to my jar:

I wish I knew how to make crème brûlée.
I wish I could grow roses.

At the time, I asked her why she was wishing for such silly things. She just poked me in the ribs and told me she already had everything she really wanted.

I'd always loved making wishes—blowing dandelion seed heads into the wind, wishing on birthday candles. I started writing some of them down because I couldn't always remember what I'd wished for and I wanted to see if any of them had actually come true. Sometimes they did. Always small wishes, though. That Mom and Dad would let me have a sleepover with a friend from school. That I'd get what I wanted for Christmas. That I wouldn't have a test or a pop quiz in history. Those kinds of things. But I could never tell if those things happened because I *wished* for them, or if it was just a coincidence.

The jar itself was an answer to one of my wishes. Sort of.

Mom and I sometimes went to garage sales on Saturday

mornings, and one morning two years ago, Mom turned as we backed out of the driveway, and met my gaze across the front seat.

"If you could find one thing today—one treasure— what would it be?"

"I wish I could find something to keep my collections in," I said.

"Good plan!" She laughed, and we pulled out of the driveway.

I really had no idea what I was looking for. An old trunk, or a small wooden container—a cigar box maybe. But when I saw a big, old mason jar, the kind that held those giant pickles at the fair, I knew it was supposed to be mine. It didn't sparkle in the sunlight or anything. It didn't call my name, and it didn't draw me irresistibly the way these kinds of things do in movies. It just sat there. But I knew it was for my wishes. I bought it for twenty-five cents and took it home, where it sat on my nightstand for three weeks, empty, while I tried to come up with a wish important enough to drop inside.

Then we found out about Mom's cancer. And I made my first wish.

As I sat in my room on the second floor of the blue house, I pulled out that no-cancer wish first, just like I always did.

I kissed it, smoothed it out, and laid it on the floor. Then I plucked the rest of the wishes from my jar one by one, the way you pull petals from a daisy.

I wish Garrett Wilson liked me.

I wish I was taller.

I wish I could play a musical instrument— something besides the recorder.

Soon, wishes lay all around me on the floor, carefully smoothed and arranged all nice and neat so I could read them. There were ones about snow days and new shoes. There were ones that made me a little embarrassed—about boys and being kissed. Wishes about things I hoped would happen. Wishes about things I hoped would *not* happen. And even wishes about wishes.

At first I'd been really particular about which wishes I put in my jar. Only the big, important ones went inside. But then I realized that every wish was important in some way. So as long as I was throwing my heart into an old glass mason jar, I might as well have some rules, because there's a difference between just hoping something will happen and intentionally wishing for it.

Rule number one: No getting rid of wishes once I had put them in the jar. This meant I had to want whatever I was wishing for badly enough to make it permanent. Of course, this made all the silly things I'd already wished for even sillier. But that didn't mean I didn't still want them to come true.

Rule number two: Only my wishes could go into the jar. I couldn't go dropping them in on behalf of someone else.

(Mom's two wishes were okay because they were already in there, and taking them out would break rule number one.)

That first wish was okay, too—that no-cancer wish—because it belonged to both Mom and me. But I couldn't say something like *I wish my dad would find the whales*. I could only say *I wish for the belugas to arrive*.

Rule number three: No hurtful wishes. I couldn't wish anyone dead or injured or anything like that, because what if it actually came true after I stopped being mad or upset with that person?

And, rule number four: All wishes had to be kept secret. I couldn't go around putting my jar on display or sharing my wishes with anyone.

When Mom died, I quit making wishes for a while. It wasn't fun anymore, not after that. Before, it had been exciting to think of things, even impossible things, to write on slips of paper and drop into my jar. Kind of like throwing a penny into a fountain and imagining your life different because of it. Because then, at least for the most part, I could pretend that my wishes didn't matter as much as everything else I already had. But after Mom was gone that changed. And now no matter what happened, everything I had left didn't feel like enough anymore.

The Little White Horse

AFTER MOM PASSED AWAY, I clung to her stories, like some kind of magical link to remember her by. She had been big into folktales. Not every night, but almost, she would pull down *Fables and Folklore from Around the World* from the impressive collection of books in our library, and we would curl up and read together. The book was great because it had all the stories I already knew, plus ones that were new and strange to me. Mom especially loved the folktales from other cultures, because she studied those kinds of things specifically.

What I remembered most clearly, though, wasn't one fairy tale or any folklore, it was what she taught me about storytelling.

"There are two kinds of stories," she said. "The kind people make up to help explain something they can't believe, and the kind people make up to help them believe something they can't explain."

My expression must have told her just how confused I was, because she'd laughed and explained it another way.

"Sometimes your mind knows that something is true, but your heart can't quite believe it. Other times it's just the opposite—when we need to believe impossible things, our hearts tell us something must be true, even when our minds tell us otherwise."

I listened carefully, watching her shape her words so that what she was trying to say came out the way she wanted.

"Everyone has to believe in something, Talia," she said. "And sometimes, instead of giving up hope, we tell stories that make the impossible possible."

But no matter how many stories Mom and I read, or how many she told me, nothing could have made it easier to hear the news about her cancer.

The week we found out was awful. Dad had to tell a lot of people at the institute because he would be taking a sabbatical at some point, just in case Mom didn't respond to treatment as well as we hoped. And everyone at school found out, too. I hadn't wanted to tell anyone about it. But in the end I didn't have to, because my teacher did it for me. There'd been no avoiding the topic after that.

"So is your Mom going to die?" one kid had asked me. I didn't even know him. He had no business asking me that question, especially when everyone was standing around watching, waiting for me to answer. But of course, it was the question we were all asking.

Later that night, when I couldn't sleep, I snuck downstairs to the library. I was too worn out and sad to do anything more than curl up with *Fables and Folklore* and get lost in someone else's story. But the door was cracked open and I found my mom already there, curled up by herself, pretending to read.

I could tell she was just pretending because her mouth wasn't moving the way it normally did. She was just staring at the open book in her lap, breathing quietly, lips still, never turning the page. I backed away from the door slowly. I didn't want to share her sadness, or make her carry mine. But the creaking of the floorboards beneath my feet gave me away.

"Tal, is that you?"

I poked my head in, and she motioned for me to join her.

Settling in next to Mom, I crossed my legs under me and spread the book across my lap. I closed my eyes and opened the book at random. This is the only proper way to choose a fairy tale—you never know if you will get the big bad wolf or Cinderella's prince.

I landed on the story of the little white horse—"The Unicorn"—and probably not by chance. This was the story I begged Mom to read most often, and we had read it so many times that *Fables and Folklore from Around the World* naturally fell open to it. I caressed the pages as if they were some kind of living thing.

I liked to tell myself I loved this story because the little white horse was so beautiful. But truthfully, I loved it because it said that unicorns granted wishes.

"I love that story," Mom said softly when she saw what I was reading.

"Me too," I said.

"I will never outgrow fairy tales," Mom sighed. "They are my very favorite kinds of stories. And almost every people group in the world has their own set of them."

"Why's that?" I asked.

She put her arm around me, pulling me close, and I rested my head on her shoulder. We curled up, soaking in the early evening sun.

"Because they tell truths about things—things people feel they need to remember," Mom said, stroking my hair. "The best stories always do."

"Will you read this to me again?" I asked, shuffling the book from my lap into hers. But she shook her head and handed it back.

"I don't need to read it, Tal," she said with a smile. "I'm pretty sure I've got this one memorized."

Closing her eyes, she leaned her head back against the wall, paused, and recited the story to me, adding mystery and magic in all the right places, with just the sound of her voice.

A long time ago, in the days of the kings, when power and wealth were sought at all cost, the worth of a granted wish could buy you a kingdom.

I watched Mom's face, her eyes closed, her eyebrows rising and falling as she brought the words to life. Seeing her like that, her face illuminated by the setting sun, hollowed and defined by its shadows, was like seeing another part of her. A deeper, secret part, and I wanted to keep it in my memory always.

One such king ruled by terror and cruelty, inflicting harm on whomever he so chose. But it came to pass in the spring of a new year, that the king fell deathly ill. It was believed that only a unicorn could grant its owner a wish so great that even a man's life would be restored. And if the fates had their way, it would take such a wish to return the king to health.

But a unicorn could only be drawn from the depths of the forest and out of hiding by a girl pure of heart. The creature could never be taken by force, but instead, it would come and lay its head in the girl's lap and forever after belong to the one it had chosen.

So by Noble decree, all young girls were subject to the king's call of duty. One after another, girls attempted to lure the unicorn, and time and again, the unicorn did not appear. With each failed attempt, the king's condition worsened. Until a young peasant named Ana took to the task, stunning all with her gentleness and grace as the unicorn emerged, claiming her as his protector.

Though Ana had been chosen, she remained under the king's command, and as such, she would be forced to offer the unicorn's wish to the king.

Part of me felt sorry for the king, as awful as he was, because I already knew how the story ended, and part of me felt sorry for myself. We both could have used a magical creature with healing powers.

In the end, Ana defied the cruel and selfish king, refusing to hand over the unicorn or the wish that had been granted to her. Instead she used it to free the magical creature, putting herself and those she loved at great risk. For the king, though sick and dying, still commanded his kingdom and could order her imprisonment, or even death.

Drawn to her as though by magic, the unicorn returned to Ana of its free will, and together the peasant girl and the little white horse restored the kingdom to the glory of ages past.

Mom opened her eyes and smiled at me, tucking a strand of hair behind my ear.

"Sometimes people want—or maybe even need—

to believe there is something out there with the power to grant them the things they desire most," she said. "Things they can't get on their own."

"Like what kind of things?" I asked. I'd never needed an answer before, but suddenly, desperately, I needed to know.

"Well, like love and health, power, hope—those kinds of things," she'd said. "The earliest mythological stories—stories that Ana's tale is based on—claimed the unicorn was beautiful and mysterious, selfless, wild, dangerous even. But always good. His horn was even believed to neutralize poison."

I glanced furtively at the bruise on the inside of my mom's arm—an ugly spot of blue and purple where chemotherapy treatment—medication and poison both—had entered her body for the first time that morning. I'd had to look away while the nurse inserted the IV that connected to a bloated bag of fluid. Standing beside Mom's hospital bed and trying my best to be brave, I had wanted nothing more in the entire world than to be that young girl from the story, pure of heart, chosen by a unicorn. I would have wished the cancer away and saved us all.

As I sat there, on the edge of the Arctic, I knew I'd never stumble across a magical little white horse—here, or anywhere. That was stupid. I knew deep down that unicorns didn't exist. And even if they did, my heart wasn't pure enough to be chosen by one.

But that didn't keep me from flipping to those familiar pages in *Fables and Folklore from Around the World* while Dad worked late and worried about his missing whales.

I read the unicorn story over and over to distract myself, buried under blankets in my bedroom on the second floor of the blue house. And even though I knew unicorns weren't real, I couldn't resist pulling out my jar of wishes every so often and slipping a wish inside, just in case. I figured that if I believed hard enough, maybe whatever truth or mystery or possibility lay in the unicorn story might be enough to do something about my wishes. If not grant them, then maybe just show me what to do next.

I woke up early on the morning of May twenty-seventh. This was it. The trip Dad had come so far to make. No more trial runs, no more day trips to test the terrain or map his route.

So I got out of bed and wrote in my neatest handwriting two brand-new wishes on their own little slips of white paper.

I wish for whales.

I wish for safe, solid ice.

Then I kissed each wish gently before dropping them in my jar with all the others.

Out on the Ice

AFTER I'D MADE MY WISHES, I went to the CNSC to watch Dad pack up the last of his gear and check his supply lists for the hundredth time. I was memorizing him so I wouldn't forget anything while he was gone. *Or in case he doesn't come back,* a small dark voice whispered in my heart.

This time, Dad would stay out on the floes until the ice started to break up, which would force him and his team back to shore.

"I'll be back the first week of July," he told me, "or maybe even earlier, depending on the ice." But that didn't change my loneliness. I was already adding up the days in my head, counting the weeks and marking the pages of Dad's pocket calendar with imaginary notes begging him to come back. I wanted to write my name on every square so he would remember I was still here.

Dad and his team would cross the frigid waters on airboats—large inflatable boats powered by giant fans that can propel them across the surface of the ice. The boats would get the team where they needed to go, even when the ice started breaking up. But I was counting on them finding whales and being back before then. It wasn't safe to be anywhere near those massive chunks of ice once they started moving. And Dad knew it.

"If a guy were to get caught out on the ice in the middle of spring breakup, he can pretty much kiss his chances of seeing dry land good-bye." Dad smiled, but there was a seriousness behind his eyes as he heaved his duffel bag over his shoulder.

It was no joke. When the floes start to break apart, the icy water underneath is only part of the danger. The little islands of ice floating and bobbing and grinding against each other can weigh as much as a house. An airboat could easily get caught between two chunks of ice and be punctured, or be dragged beneath the surface, or even worse, flipped, sending everyone and everything aboard into dark, icy waters. In this kind of work you had to be much more than just a researcher. You had to be an arctic explorer, an expert seaman, a survivalist, and an adventurer all rolled into one.

I tried to tell myself not to worry. *He's done this before, lots of times. And so has his team. Everything will be fine. He'll be back before you know it.*

I repeated this over and over while I stood on shore with Sura, watching them load the boats, lash down gear, and secure themselves against the wind. They loaded in food supplies, fuel, tents, water-resistant clothing and blankets, and crate after crate of research equipment. And when everything was arranged just the way Dad liked it, he walked back across the rocks to where I stood on the shoreline, my arms wrapped around myself for warmth.

Dad stood there for a minute, and then pulled me tight against his chest like he was trying to squeeze the sadness right out of us both.

"I'm sorry, Talia," he said quietly. "I'm sorry to leave you." I wrapped my arms even tighter around him, trying to shrink that Mom-sized space. He kissed the top of my hair and pulled away, but I didn't let go of his coat.

"I'll be back soon," he said, holding my face in his mittened hands. "Promise."

Dad blinked several times and cleared his throat. I swallowed hard, working to keep my tears inside, and then I let go.

"I'll call you once we're out," he said, patting the radio belted to his waist.

We'd arranged weekly call-ins. On Sunday evenings, Dad would radio in to check on me and let me know how things were going. I would know he was safe. And he would know I was doing okay.

"Thank you, Sura." Dad turned to her, and she smiled.

"Take care," she said. "And don't worry about anything back here. We will be just fine."

Just fine. I let those words sit with me for a minute. What did they mean anyway? What did it mean to be just fine? Nothing about this felt fine. But I didn't have time to figure out an answer before Dad pressed his lips to my forehead one more time and then was gone, walking back over the shore and into one of the airboats.

The giant propeller fans roared to life, stirring up blinding swirls of snow. The blades were housed in a kind of cage, just like the tabletop fan I used at home when the weather was hot. The small crowd that had gathered on the shoreline backed away, and I shielded my face with my mittened hands, shutting out the cold, the wind, and the sight of my dad leaving me.

Sura and I stood there a while longer, not saying anything. And when my dad was finally, truly gone, and even the tiny dark specks of his team had vanished over the horizon line, Sura and I walked back to the blue house.

I didn't really want her there. I didn't want to have to pretend I was okay with all of this. I didn't have anything to say, and I wanted to be alone, though I knew it wouldn't help. But Sura didn't say anything as we walked; she just let me be quiet. I think maybe she knew how empty words can be sometimes.

As we walked, our breath hung suspended around us in

tiny clouds and the snow squeaked under our boots. It was so cold that all the moisture had been sucked out of the snow until only tiny bits of ice remained—broken bits of snowflakes. Like grains of frozen sand, they gave way under my feet, making me clumsy and slow.

When we got back to the house, Sura paused on the porch for a minute, and then she went inside and let me be.

I wandered around outside for a while, not wanting to go in and face all the space my dad had left behind. Eventually, the wind and ice and snow forced me up the porch stairs and into the house. No one can stay out in the cold forever, and I was no exception.

Unicorns of the Sea

IT WAS WARM AND QUIET inside, and I paused in the entryway, letting the warmth wash over me before I hung up my coat and unlaced my boots. Sura stood in the kitchen, stirring a small pot of hot chocolate over the stove, and she turned, smiling, as I came in.

"Cold?" she asked.

I nodded, chewing the ends of my hair.

She handed me a blue mug and I wrapped my fingers around it, letting the warmth seep in. Leaning against the counter, I sipped, careful not to burn my tongue, and we stood there in the kitchen for a few minutes, listening to the radiator clunk and gurgle.

"You are her daughter," Sura said, leaning against the counter across the kitchen from me. "In many ways, you are her daughter."

Her words were soft, but she might as well have shouted them at me. It made me uncomfortable to hear Sura mention my mom.

I took a deep breath, running my fingers around the spiraling white handle of my mug, tracing its shape from base to lip. It was exactly like the horn of a unicorn, only curved, tight against the back of my hand where I'd curled my fingers around the mug.

"They met here," Sura said. "Did you know that?"

I shook my head. I wondered why they never told me.

"Katherine was doing her thesis on oral culture and storytelling, and your dad was here researching whales. My mother was alive then—Ahana. She was one of our elders." Sura shrugged. "Churchill is much different from a traditional Inuit village now. Modern. But our people are the same, and some of our traditions are the same. We tell a lot of stories, and my mother was a storyteller."

"So was mine," I said, and Sura nodded.

"She stayed here with my mother and me to learn about our culture. She would sit here and listen to Ahana—learning things we can only teach through stories."

"What sort of stories did she tell? Your mom, I mean." It was so strange, standing here in Sura's kitchen, knowing my mom had been here, too, a long time ago.

"Oh, all kinds—'Why the Stars Are in the Sky,' 'Crow Brings Daylight,' 'The Fox Wife,' 'How the Raven Became Black,' 'The Unicorn of the Sea'—"

"What?" I sputtered into my hot chocolate and nearly dropped the cup. "What about a unicorn?"

Sura jumped up and handed me a napkin. I hadn't told anyone about the stories Mom read to me, and the last thing I expected was to hear anything about unicorns way out here in the frozen Arctic.

"'The Unicorn of the Sea.' It's an old Inuit tale. But if you ever find one, close your eyes. Tight," Sura said. "Unicorns break your heart."

I frowned, setting my hot chocolate on the kitchen counter and wiping my mouth.

"What does that mean?" I asked.

She didn't say anything for a minute, and then sat down.

"Would you like to hear the story?"

I nodded and joined her at the table. Fast. Too fast. But my knees had gone all wobbly and the tips of my fingers were tingling.

"There are a couple different versions of this story," Sura began. "But I will tell you my favorite."

As Sura spoke, I was certain I heard the wishes in my jar start to shift and rustle around.

"Many, many years ago there was an Inuit girl who fell in love with the sea," Sura said. "Every day she would go out on the water with her father, who was a hunter, and beg him to spare the whales. And because he loved his daughter, he did. But the Inuit people needed the whales," Sura said, "and without them, they began to starve."

I remembered Dad telling me about all of the ways the Inuit people used the whales they hunted. They would eat the whale meat of course, but they would also eat the fat, or blubber, because it is so rich in nutrients. Other times they would melt down the blubber into oil to use as fuel for light. They even used the bones, boiling them into glue and grinding them down for fertilizer. In fact, bones and teeth can be carved into tools and shaped into special hooks for fishing nets.

I knew this was a way of life for the Inuit, but it was a lot different from mine. Different than what I was used to. It seemed cruel. I understood why that girl didn't want her dad to kill those whales.

"Even though the people were going hungry and growing ill," Sura continued, "the hunter's daughter still begged her father to spare the whales. And so he spared them, until his daughter also grew weak and sick for lack of food. And then, because he loved her more than he loved her happiness, the girl's father took his harpoon and went out to hunt the whales.

"But the girl, who did not understand either the sea she loved or her father who loved them both, tied herself to his harpoon. Her father never knew, and when he cast it out, his daughter was dragged into the sea.

"The father's grief was so great that the sea took pity on him, and the girl did not drown. Instead, with the harpoon held tightly in her hands, she was bound to a beluga whale.

Tangled in the ropes of the harpoon, and wrapped around one another, together they became the unicorn of the sea. Today, they are known as narwhals."

Sura paused.

"But unicorns break your heart, Talia," she said, and this time she said it firmly, like a warning. "The girl loved what she could not have. She was permanently changed, more creature than human. And it broke her father's heart. They were separated from each other forever."

Sura looked sad.

"But she saved the whales, didn't she?" I sat in my chair, thinking about the story and listening to my wishes rustle in their jar. "That was what she wanted more than anything."

Sura nodded thoughtfully.

"So maybe that was enough for her. Maybe it didn't matter that she was separated from her father. Maybe they were already kind of separated before she was changed because they were so different, and maybe she was actually happier with the whales." In my mind, all I could see was the gray mottled body of a narwhal whale and the single spiraling horn that rose up out of the water like the lance of a jousting knight.

"Perhaps she was." Sura smiled. "There is a piece of truth in all stories. Including this one. Those pieces make stories magic, which is part of the reason the Inuit tell them over and over, generation after generation. The pieces we choose to keep, to make our own, change us. They change the way we live and think, and what we believe. Perhaps the girl was happier as one of the whales. Or perhaps she wished she could return to her father." Sura shrugged. "Whichever piece of truth you choose to remember will change how you hear the story. And it will change *you*, too. It's magic."

Magic unicorns or magic stories, I wasn't quite sure which one rang the most true to me, but I had no trouble believing that the things you chose to take away from a story could change everything.

I knew from one of Dad's excited rants that during medieval times people thought the narwhal's horn, which is actually a tusk, was the horn of a unicorn. They didn't realize it came from a whale. And Vikings and other northern traders thought the horn was incredibly valuable. They exchanged the narwhal's tusk for gold and even believed it had magical powers. Cups were carved out of tusks for important people, like kings and queens, who believed drinking from them destroyed poison. Even Queen Elizabeth of England bought a narwhal tusk for as much as it would've cost her to purchase a *castle*. She used it as a scepter. I wondered if Sura knew about any of that.

Before, no matter how much I wanted the magical stories about the little white horse to be real, I knew I couldn't possibly wish the creature into existence.

But out here, where the winter sky glowed with the pale light of the aurora borealis, and where the frozen Arctic Sea was mysterious and alive beneath the ice, and where the Inuit people tell old, magic stories—out here, unicorns were *real*.

And somewhere between the stories that help explain something people can't believe and the stories that help them believe something they can't explain, there was just enough truth to make me hope for something crazy—something *impossible*.

I excused myself from the table and left Sura to finish her hot chocolate alone, then bolted up the stairs to my room. Throwing myself to the floor, I pulled out my jar from beneath the bed.

With shaking fingers I drew out that first wish, the same way I always did. Then one by one, plucking out the rest, I smoothed and read them, almost too excited to bear it. But I needed to go slow. *Deep breaths.* This was too important.

Finally, when the jar was empty, I took out a pencil and a little slip of paper from the bedside table drawer, and I made another wish. The biggest wish I'd ever made.

All this time I'd been hoping if I believed hard enough in the stories I already knew—in the stories Mom had told me—that the mysterious possibility or secret truth hiding in them would be enough to make them come true. And now, way out here on the edge of the Arctic, I'd finally found what I was looking for. I'd found the spark that would bring them to life.

I'd been waiting for unicorns all along—I'd just been waiting for the wrong ones.

A plan was starting to form in the back of my mind.

I had to see one for myself. I had to get out on open Arctic waters and wait for that spiraling white horn to rise up out of the sea.

It was risky, planning around something as rare as a narwhal whale, but if the unicorns in my mom's stories could grant wishes, maybe the unicorns of the sea could, too. And if there was even the tiniest hope that this was possible, then I would take it.

I chewed on the end of my pencil, staring out the window from where I sat on my bedroom floor. Sura would probably be up to check on me before long. I'd left her sitting at the kitchen table without much of an explanation. I hadn't even thanked her for the story or the hot chocolate.

I sighed and started picking up my wishes. The last thing I needed was for Sura to walk in on me with my wishes spread out all over the floor. So one by one I kissed them, and dropped them back inside until my jar was full of paper slips again. Only my newest wish still lay beside me.

I set my pencil down and rolled it across the floorboards, watching as it came to a slow stop against my jar. I studied my newest wish. It felt heavier than the rest, like it would fall through the air faster than the others if I dropped them all at the same time.

I stared at it, fresh and crisp against the dingy floorboards, my handwriting firm and deliberate across the white paper. And then I gently picked it up and kissed it, before dropping it inside with all the others.

The Guitar Boy and the Birdman

THE AIR ON THE FRONT porch was crisp and clear, freezing as it left my body and hung around my head in a glittering cloud. I narrowed my lips and blew a stream into the morning air, leaning against the porch rail and staring out across the frozen surface of Hudson Bay.

I couldn't see any trace of them—Dad and his team—not even tracks in the snow where the airboats had propelled them over the ice just a few days ago. The wind had blown away any evidence that they had ever been there. It was ruthless like that, carving away the landscape, never bothered by ice, or snow, or people's lives. It pushed drifts halfway up the north side of the blue house, and at the same time, swept the surface of Hudson Bay smooth as glass.

This was a strange place. Cold and empty, and if you weren't paying attention, you might think it never changed. But you would be wrong. It changed constantly. This was something I was just starting to figure out. I'd spent enough time staring out my bedroom window to finally see it.

Some things were obvious, like the way the snow shifted under the relentless wind. There was the ice, solid and thick enough to drive cars and trucks across if you wanted. But eventually, it would break apart under the gentle force of the sun, or so Sura told me. And then there were the changes that had happened long ago, long before I was here and even before the Inuit. Maybe only Dad's little white whales were around to witness it—the massive movement of glaciers carving away the landscape and leaving moraine in their wake.

I hunched deeper into my heavy coat, trying not to think about the fact that Dad had only been gone for three days. It made time drag on as slowly as a glacier. That's what I was doing—trying not to think about the weeks and weeks between today and when Dad would eventually come in off the ice—when I heard faint strains of music drifting across the tundra. Turning, I watched as a boy came walking past the blue house.

No. Not walking. He was practically *dancing*. Kind of

rocking and swaying, and strumming a guitar. The Guitar Boy singing Bob Dylan in the middle of the frozen, snowy street. I craned my neck to get a better look at him as he strolled by, singing and playing, his breath sparkling around him. I recognized the song immediately as one of my mom's favorites: "It's All Over Now Baby Blue."

He couldn't have been much older than me, straight and tall with a shock of blond hair sticking up off one side of his head. He reminded me of the spruce trees that grew here, their branches clinging to only one side because of the constant driving cold and ice.

He was underdressed. It was relatively warm today—thirty-three degrees Fahrenheit—but still. In place of the typical Churchill uniform of a thick parka and fur-lined boots, he wore an army green peacoat, unbuttoned over a lopsided gray sweater someone had probably made for him. He wore sturdy boots laced up loosely over the hem of his jeans, barely keeping the snow out, and fingerless gloves that couldn't possibly have kept out the cold. It couldn't have been easy to play the guitar in those gloves, either.

He was nearly a block past me when he finished his song, whirled around, and caught me staring. Then he bowed.

You're supposed to bow with one arm folded at your back and one folded against your stomach. I knew this because our band teacher always insisted we bow after our school concerts, and she was pretty specific on how it was done. But not that boy. He bowed deeply, one hand grasping the neck of his guitar, the other flung out behind him.

I didn't know what else to do, so I bowed back. But just a bit.

This boy was the strangest thing I'd seen since arriving in Churchill, which was saying something. And yet, he seemed to belong here, too. If I'd been at home and that boy had come waltzing down the street in front of our apartment with his guitar, I probably would have laughed. But not here. Here, he fit. And it was all I could do to keep from jumping off the porch steps and following him wherever he was going. It was like that old story—I felt like one of those children of Hamelin, wanting to follow the pied piper out of the city.

"His name is Simon," Sura told me later over lunch. "He's the Birdman's grandson. The two of them come to Churchill every summer."

I chewed my sandwich thoughtfully.

"The Birdman?"

I took a gulp of milk. It seemed a funny thing to call someone. I pictured a comfortably fat, elderly gentleman with round glasses, a large nose, and very long legs.

"He collects birds," Sura replied.

I added a giant net and a birdcage to the picture growing in my mind.

"The Birdman is a researcher, Tal, like your father," Sura

continued. "An ornithologist. He makes lists and writes descriptions of all the birds he's observed and studied."

"And what about Simon?" I asked. The guitar and that boy's easy bow waved in my memory like a welcome flag. It was like he just didn't care what anyone thought of him. I never would have done that, even if I had a good reason to.

"Simon is . . ." Sura trailed off and then reached out and patted my hand. "Why don't you go find out? Are you done?"

I nodded, swallowing the last bite of my sandwich. She took my plate and began washing up our lunch dishes.

I knew I should stay and help. Offer to dry or something. But I didn't want to. Sura and I were getting along pretty well, considering. Still, it wasn't like we were best friends or anything. I didn't want to stand beside her at the sink and pretend.

"Go on." She nodded to the door and smiled.

She didn't have to tell me twice.

Churchill might be a small town, but it was still unfamiliar to me. Fortunately, many of the locals seemed to know each other, so I had a good feeling that if I got lost, all I had to do was tell someone where I was staying and I'd probably get a guided tour of Churchill all the way back to the blue house.

I wandered around town for a while, trying to catch a glimpse of the boy with the guitar and feeling like a spy. This wasn't the sort of thing I would normally do. But then, there was nothing normal about this whole thing—me being here and Dad being gone, this frozen place, that boy.

I stopped at the post office to pick up our mail and chat with the woman behind the counter. I thought the boy might be there. But he wasn't. Then I wandered over to a restaurant called the Hub and ordered a hot chocolate, even though I'd just had one.

"Hello, Talia," Meryl, the owner, greeted me cheerfully. Loudly. The other diners turned to glance in our direction. I didn't like being the center of attention. But Meryl did, and in her restaurant, she always was.

Meryl ran a damp cloth across the counter, scattering leftover crumbs from the previous diner's meal. I thought about doing the same thing—scattering. But I gritted my teeth and remained sitting.

"Hi," I said, sipping my hot chocolate and scanning the people who'd returned to their lunch.

Meryl made it her business to know everything about everyone in Churchill. Dad and I hadn't been here for more than a few days before she dropped by Sura's house with a plate of cinnamon rolls. Meryl was a big woman—she filled a room with her presence and her voice. Really, she was no taller or wider than Sura, but she always made me feel swallowed up.

"Are you meeting someone?" She cocked an eyebrow at me, leaning her elbow against the counter. Dad and I had come here together our first week in Churchill, but I'd never come by myself.

"No." I shook my head, trying to look mature, like I went to restaurants by myself all the time. "I was just thirsty."

I wished Meryl would go away. She didn't. Instead she followed my gaze around the room as I searched for a shock of blond hair sticking up off just one side. But he wasn't there, and I drank my hot chocolate too fast, burning my tongue and the roof of my mouth.

Meryl winked at me as I paid for my drink. She knew that nobody came to the Hub just for food. Everyone came for the company. Even me. Churchill, Manitoba, was too cold and too far away from the rest of the world for people to pretend that they didn't need each other.

Tugging my hat down over my ears, I stepped back out into the cold, feeling more alone than before. It was silly. I didn't even know Simon, or anything about him. So I had no reason to feel any different than I had before. But I did. I felt like I'd missed out on something. He seemed like the sort of person who would be fun to be around.

I took the side streets toward the blue house, dragging my feet in the dirty snow until I found the gravel road that ran along the edge of town. This eventually wound along the shore, and though it was sort of a long walk, I wanted to look at the frozen bay before going back. Sura would worry if I was gone too long, but the bay tugged at me. My dad was out there somewhere, standing on its frozen surface, looking for whales. The wind pushed at my back, urging me along, and every now and then I scanned the scrub brush for the off chance that a polar bear was there, waiting for an afternoon snack to come along.

Rounding a small bend in the road, I could see the curve of the shore stretching out ahead until it met the mouth of the Churchill River. And I was so busy tracing that curve of shoreline I almost ran straight into the Birdman.

He was standing in the middle of the road, and I *knew* it was him, though I couldn't say how I knew. It was just that he couldn't have been anyone else. He wasn't fat at all, but wonderfully fit, like a runner. His hair was salt-and-pepper gray and he had a long mustache, which curled up at the ends just a little, making him look happy even if he wasn't smiling. A small pair of binoculars hung around his neck.

I was about to say hello when he raised a finger to his lips and pointed. He was aiming just over my left shoulder into the scrub. Slowly, he brought his binoculars to his face. I froze, caught in the crosshairs of a fantastic observation.

"Northern Wheatear," he said, his voice low. I didn't know if that was a good thing or not, but I didn't dare move. I barely even breathed.

At last, he lowered the binoculars.

"Come, have a look," he said.

I relaxed, curious, and took the binoculars he offered, holding them to my face. With some help, I found the nondescript little bird, teetering on the sparse limb of a black spruce.

"Notice the inverted black *T* along its tail," the Birdman pointed out.

I noticed and nodded, and we both watched until the little bird flew away into the scrub. Reluctantly, I returned the binoculars.

"Talia Lea McQuinn," I said, sticking out my hand, and he took it with a surprised grin. "And you're the Birdman," I finished with certainty.

He threw back his head and laughed, and for a minute I wondered if anyone actually called him that directly. Maybe they just called him the Birdman when they were talking *about* him.

"Why, yes. Yes, I guess I am the Birdman," he said. "It's very nice to meet you, Talia Lea McQuinn."

"Tal," I said.

"Tal," he agreed.

And that was that.

Good

I WOKE UP THE NEXT morning with a terrible cold. My throat ached, I could hardly breathe, and every part of me hurt. I felt as if a polar bear had tried to snack on me during the night. Groaning, I pulled the covers over my head and rolled over, trying to fall back asleep.

Under the covers in the muffled darkness, I tried thinking about cool, calm waters, hoping they might lull me back to sleep. Then Sura knocked and opened the door.

"Are you all right, Tal? It's almost eleven o'clock."

"I'm sick," I said, poking my head out from under the covers. My voice was funny, like it was stuck in my head.

Sura came in and sat on the edge of my bed, pressed a cool hand to my forehead. A rush of memory washed over me, and the room heaved like the deck of a wave-tossed ship.

My mom had always been quick to press her hands against

my face—when I was sick; when my cheeks were cold and rosy from being out in the wind; when they were warm and her hands cold; when she wanted me to know I was loved.

I jerked away from Sura's hands and she pulled back, standing up awkwardly.

My small room seemed to shrink even smaller and I wanted to pull myself back under the covers like a turtle.

I knew Sura was just trying to be nice, but it only reminded me that Mom was gone all over again. Homemade pancakes for breakfast. Hot chocolate on a cold afternoon. A cool hand against my hot forehead. And what if Mom was watching? What if she knew?

"I'll bring you some tea and toast," Sura said. But I just nodded and didn't look at her.

Sura was the perfect sort of mom person, even though she wasn't anyone's mom. She wasn't even anyone's wife. I'd never thought about that before, and it suddenly made me a bit uncomfortable. Because, what if she wanted to be? Maybe she would have liked to be someone's wife? Someone's mom? She was already pretty good at taking care of other people, though I knew from experience that you didn't have to be a mom to learn how to do that.

I was only eleven when Dad and I started taking care of Mom. I knew then that she wasn't going to get better. The three of us never talked about it, at least, not like we talked about other things. And we never talked about the future at all—about what we'd do *after*.

The truth was, I was terrified. I didn't know how we would ever be okay without her. *Everyone is afraid of what they're unable to control*, Mom had told me. *All fears can eventually be traced back to that.* It made sense, what she said. But it didn't make me feel any better.

I knew Mom loved me, but she and Dad weren't the sort of people who went around saying so all the time. Instead, they showed it in hundreds of little ways. It never really bothered me, until the cancer. Once Mom was diagnosed, it would've been nice to have those three little words inside me somewhere, so I could anchor myself to them when the waves really rolled.

The day I realized things had flipped—that Mom was no longer taking care of me—wasn't anything I could have prepared for. And it wasn't just because of the cancer; it was the drugs, too. There would be no more chemotherapy. No more radiation. There would be just Dad, and me, and Mom. And morphine.

Dad told me that morphine is a pretty wild breed of pain-killer, and toward the end, when she came home from the hospital, Mom was hooked up to an IV that fed her a constant drip of that particular wild breed.

"It helps with the pain," Dad said. But it didn't help mine at all.

It was a late October afternoon, and Mom was propped up by pillows next to the big picture window in the library. She liked the sunshine, so we turned our story room into her bedroom.

I was doing homework at the desk beside her bed, and I had a terrible cold. I remember the balled-up tissues on the floor and how my nose hurt from blowing. Dad had gone into work to wrap up a report after I got home from school. He had arranged for a nurse to come and check on Mom every afternoon—but she wouldn't be there for a couple more hours. So it was just Mom and me, cozied up like a couple of cats in the warm autumn sunshine that poured through the library window.

Out of the blue, Mom asked me a question I knew I would never forget.

"Have I been a good mom, Tal?"

I glanced up from my homework, a little confused by her question. At first I thought it was the morphine talking. Mom wasn't the sort of person ever to be uncertain about things, at least, not to me. Before cancer she never would've asked me that sort of question. I put down my pencil.

"The best," I said. I didn't even have to think about it. "You're the best." I said it again because I didn't want her to have to think about it, either. Why hadn't I ever told her this before? I guess sometimes you over-look things because they seem so obvious.

I got up from my desk and went to lie beside Mom, trying my best not to hurt her. I traced the bright blue veins in her thin hands. They looked like the twisting lines on a road map, and I wished that we could all just drive away and leave the whole broken and sick world behind.

I don't know how long we lay there together, but when I looked over, Mom had fallen asleep. The mor-phine made her do that—fall asleep really fast. I didn't want to wake her, but I needed her to know, so I whis-pered, "I love you."

Dad found us there in the library when he got home later that night. Mom and I were both asleep. And when she woke up, she didn't seem to remember any of our conversation. Or if she did, she never said anything.

She died a week later, while I was at school.

The school secretary called me out of class to the princi-pal's office. He didn't need words to tell me what had hap-pened; his face told me the truth I didn't want to know. I remember slowly packing up my books as the class watched, my hands shaking.

It's funny the things you remember. I knew I wouldn't finish my math homework that night, and I remember wondering if I should talk to my teacher about it before I left. But I didn't. I just slid my pre-algebra book into my backpack and zipped it up, the noise filling the silent classroom. Then I made my way down the long hall to where my dad waited, red-eyed and broken.

He pulled me into his arms and held me so tight I could barely breathe. And then he cried, right there in the principal's office—big gasping sobs. I remember how the principal looked down at his shoes, scuffed across the toes, and rubbed his forehead. I felt sorry for him, and embarrassed for us. Sometimes it's hard to know how to help people who are all broken up, right there in front of you.

I wanted to cry, too. I knew exactly what was happening. Mom was gone, and all the things I loved most about her were suddenly just memories. No one would ever get to know her like I knew her. I'd never be able to say, "You have *got* to meet my mom. She's super cool," because she was dead. I tried to cry because it seemed wrong, cruel almost, to let Dad stand there and do it alone. But I couldn't. I couldn't cry because I was too angry.

They had made me go to school that day, even though the nurse said she could go at any time. Mom and Dad had made me go, and now Mom had died without giving me a chance to say good-bye. The tears were there, drowning me from the inside out. But the weight of my silent good-bye kept getting in the way, keeping my eyes dry. It was like a wall.

I didn't get to say good-bye. I didn't get to say good-bye. I didn't get to say good-bye.

Those words kept repeating in my head, over and over, and no matter how hard my tears crashed against my insides, they couldn't get out. I couldn't manage a single tear, not even at Mom's funeral, which I barely remember.

After it was all over, my heart finally caught up with my head, squeezed around that absent good-bye, and down inside where I was most real, I knew she was truly gone. Then Niagara opened up in me.

I cried at the breakfast table when Dad tried to make oatmeal for us, because he didn't really know how to do it. I cried getting dressed for school because Mom wasn't there to tell me how nice I looked or to make sure my socks matched. I cried in the lunchroom at school and didn't care who saw me because it didn't matter what people thought anymore. I cried doing my homework because Mom wasn't there to help, and I cried myself to sleep at night because she wasn't there to tuck me in. Mom wasn't there, and she never would be again.

And then, as fast as it had started, it stopped. Like a faucet finally turning off. I didn't stop on purpose, the tears just quit coming, and I was relieved.

I haven't cried since.

Not when we sold our house in town and moved to an apartment close to the institution.

Not when my cat got hit by a car right after Christmas.

Not when I didn't get asked to the middle school dance.

I just couldn't imagine a reason to cry over anything else. And even if I could, I wouldn't let myself. I refused. *Nothing* could ever be that bad again.

I must have fallen asleep, because a while later I woke up to the sound of creaking floors. Sura pushed my bedroom door open with her shoulder, and it whined on its hinges. She carried a tray of tea and warm toast, and though I didn't want to admit it, it smelled *perfect*. Sitting up in bed, I pulled my pillow up behind me, and Sura set the tray on my lap.

"You may find the tea different than what you're used to, but it will help," she said. "I added honey, to sweeten it up."

I peered down into the cup of golden liquid. "What is it?"

"*Chaithluk* tea."

"Chaithluk?" I asked.

She nodded. "Stinkweed. A bit like chamomile, but the plant grows here on the tundra. It will help your throat and fever." She rubbed her arms to demonstrate. "Take the ache away."

I nodded, nervous, and took a tentative sip. It was bitter. But only at first. And it did make my throat feel a little better.

Sura stood beside the bed, watching. But she didn't touch me and she didn't sit down. As she turned to go, I caught her sleeve.

"Thanks," I said. "This is nice."

Sura nodded, accepting the compliment. Then she left me in my room with only my thoughts for company.

Miss Piggy

SATURDAY MORNING, I MET THE Guitar Boy. Officially.

Plodding down the stairs, rubbing sleep from my eyes, I found him at the breakfast table eating pancakes as fast as Sura could flip them. His guitar hung over the back of his chair where he'd taken it off, like the way a man removes his hat in church. Sura and Simon were laughing—his warm and boyish, and hers as warm and rich as the hot chocolate she made. Her eyes squinted up all tiny when she laughed, and I stood on the step, watching, confused.

They *knew* each other.

I'd assumed Sura just knew *of* Simon. But they talked like people who've known each other for a long time. And she hadn't told me anything about him. Not a single thing. She just let me wander off the other day and go looking for him.

That lonely feeling was creeping into my chest again, forming a lump in my throat.

I chewed on the ends of my hair, wanting to run back up to my room. I turned on the stair, hoping I could creep up quietly without them noticing. But Sura must have heard me. She cleared her throat, and I turned to find a setting at the table where she'd laid a place for me.

"Come and eat, Tal," she said, pulling me down the stairs with her smile and a plate of homemade pancakes. I sighed and reluctantly came down into the warm kitchen.

On the stairs I'd been an observer, but as I stood there trying to decide where I fit in this room, the blue house curled itself around me, pulling me in. Everything smelled like maple syrup and hot coffee. Guitars, sweaters the color of saffron, and red hats belonged. The cold frozenness of the Arctic wasn't allowed inside.

I slipped into the chair across from Simon, a little uncomfortable. He passed the bottle of syrup without comment. His hair was behaving itself today. I liked it better sticking up off one side.

I watched as Sura turned pancakes at the stove, smiling. I was beginning to realize that Sura used her cooking to show people how she felt about them. It was kind of nice.

I didn't say much all through breakfast, which seemed to be okay with Simon. The Guitar Boy was alive and animated, making up for my silence by talking and singing continually, telling about his year, his friends, and his grandfather. His life seemed like some kind of grand performance, and it made my life seem pretty boring by comparison. I thought about that sweeping bow he'd made the first time I saw him. It made more sense now. It fit him. He had a song for *everything*, and when he couldn't find one, he made one up.

As I finished eating, the Guitar Boy pushed himself away from the table and slung his guitar back over his shoulder where it belonged. He kissed Sura on the cheek, thanking her for breakfast, and then nodded toward the door.

"C'mon, *you*," he said to me. "We're going to visit Miss Piggy."

I waited for a minute, expecting some kind of explanation, but he just stood there, looking at me.

"I have a *name*, you know." I couldn't think of anything else to say.

The Guitar Boy grinned, unfazed, and as if that had been some kind of invitation, he swung his guitar around and broke into song. Something about names, and that everyone and everything has one.

Strumming a final chord, he closed with that sweeping bow of his—one arm flung out behind him. This time I clapped. He seemed like the sort of person you needed to clap for. And besides that, he was actually pretty good. Even though I'd only ever played the recorder for band, I could recognize talent when I heard it.

"Talia Lea McQuinn," I said, standing up and sticking out my hand, just like I'd done with his grandfather.

"Yes," he said. "I know." And he took my hand. But instead of the shake I expected, he bent over and kissed it, the way men do in old movies. I snatched it away and jammed both hands deep into the pockets of my flannel pajama pants.

Laughing, he thumbed toward the door. "I'll wait here. You should probably get dressed."

Of course, if I'd known he was coming for breakfast, I would've. This wasn't the sort of first impression I'd had in mind—me in my pajamas. But I just nodded, taking the stairs two at a time.

Long underwear, wool socks, jeans, and two sweaters later, I pulled my coat from its hook on the wall, laced up my boots, and waved good-bye to Sura. Then I followed the Guitar Boy out into the arctic morning.

The average temperature for Churchill this time of year ranged anywhere from three degrees below zero to thirty degrees above. Today it was on the colder side of that range and I was thankful for my layers.

"So, who is your Muppet friend?" I asked.

The Guitar Boy smiled and with a kick, sent a little chunk of ice skittering down the road. I walked beside him, my mittened hands in my pockets and my red hat pulled down over my ears. The wind pushed at our backs as we trudged down the road, cold, but not unkind.

"You'll see." The Guitar Boy grinned at me, secretive.

I glanced away, burying my hands deeper into my coat pockets and peered anxiously into the scrub. Surprises made me uncomfortable, and I was terrified we were going to get one from a bear.

I fell in step a little ways behind Simon. I kept pausing to listen for growling noises, or the sound of branches breaking, just in case something was trying to sneak up on us.

After we'd gone a bit farther, he stopped and turned around. "Come on already!"

"Coming," I said, glancing up. I wasn't sure what I'd do if I actually saw a bear. I read once that if you were ever attacked by a bear, you're supposed to drop down and cover the back of your head with your arms. But this seemed pretty stupid to me. In theory, it was supposed to protect the most vital parts of your body. But I figured if a bear was interested in any of my vital parts, covering the back of my head with my hands wasn't going to make much of a difference.

Simon waited while I scrambled up after him, carefully navigating a pile of rocks. We'd left the road, but the foot-path we were on seemed well traveled enough.

"I doubt we'll see any," the Guitar Boy said. "Bears, I mean."

Dad told me my face was easier to read than the alphabet, and I frowned. Simon seemed to know exactly what I was thinking, and that was a little embarrassing.

"How do you know?" I asked. "How do you know we

won't see any . . . bears?" I lowered my voice at the end in case they were listening and felt inclined to investigate.

The Guitar Boy seemed pretty confident, but I wasn't that trusting.

"It's too early," he said, readjusting his guitar strap.

"Yeah, but what if we do? You don't have a gun or *anything*." Somewhere in the darker corners of my imagination, I was terrified I'd die beneath the claws and teeth of nanuq.

"Not true." The Guitar Boy paused, digging into his pocket, and tossed me a small black canister.

I caught it clumsily and turned it over. "Are you *serious*?"

The small red-and-yellow label read *Mace*. The Guitar Boy laughed at my skepticism and continued on ahead.

I should have just left it at "gun." He didn't have a gun. End of story. Pepper spray didn't make me feel any safer. And now I didn't know whether to try and find my way back alone or follow him. We were out in the middle of nowhere, about to walk right between a mother bear and her cubs for all I knew. I've heard this is about as close to a death wish as a person could get, and our only defense was a can of Mace. Suddenly, I wanted to pick up the pace.

"Here—maybe you should hang on to it." I hurried after Simon, thrusting the Mace into his hand, and he shoved it back into his pocket before throwing his arm over my shoulder.

"Don't you worry," he said. "I've got you covered."

We walked for another half hour or so with no sign of bears, and then finally, cresting a little rise, I got my first look at Miss Piggy.

"There she is." The Guitar Boy nodded.

"So, not a Muppet," I said.

"Nope. Not a Muppet. An airplane. Or what's left of an airplane. An old Curtiss C-46 Commando. She was operated by Lamb Air back in the sixties and seventies," he said. "She crashed when her left engine failed just outside of Churchill in 1979. The wreck is a pretty big deal here. People visit the site all the time."

"Why is she called Miss Piggy?"

"Because she was able to carry so much freight," he said. "And because at one time, she actually hauled a load of pigs. Or so the story goes."

I wrinkled my nose. That couldn't have been a pleasant flight.

"She used to be red and white," the Guitar Boy said. "But one side of her was painted gray several years ago when she was used as part of a movie set."

Miss Piggy had crashed on the edge of a rise, in a pile of glacial rock. Her wings were barely attached to her body, collapsing down the slope. She looked like a giant bird splayed across the ground. And suddenly, I wanted to reassemble her pieces and send her back into the sky where she belonged.

As Simon and I climbed up one of the wings, making our way toward the empty cockpit, my excitement faded and a sort of uneasy weight settled in my chest. Hunching my shoulders, I ducked my chin into my coat collar, shielding myself against the cold. Mom always said I had an overactive imagination. And I don't think she thought it was a good thing. At the time it made me mad, because really, what's so bad about an overactive imagination? But she was probably right, because I had a tendency to scare myself.

As the wind blew up over the rise, I was certain I heard the frantic voices of Miss Piggy's crew echoing in the hollowed-out belly of the plane. The grinding gears of a failing engine screeched in my ears, and in my mind, I saw the plane plummet toward the ground. I shivered and rubbed my arms.

The inside of the plane was completely empty, its naked spars and ribs curving up over my head. I felt like Jonah inside the belly of a whale.

People had been here with paint cans and sprayed graffiti across the floor and along the walls. But I couldn't read any of it because it was in a different language. Inuktitut probably. What was so important that someone needed to say it here, in paint, in the hollowed-out belly of a plane wreck?

Simon jumped into the cockpit and hunched over the empty face of the control panel. Buttons and dials, the instruments, everything was gone—gutted and hollowed out by time and the curiosity of tourists. Even the pilot's and copilot's seats were gone. I stood where the copilot's seat had once been bolted to the floor, and stared out the glassless windshield over the rock-strewn tundra.

Grabbing an imaginary wheel, Simon pulled an imaginary radio from the ceiling.

"Mayday. Mayday. Mayday," he said, his voice urgent. "This is pilot Simon Wendell, C-46 Commando with Lamb Air. We've lost pressure in our left engine. Requesting immediate assistance."

I blinked, feeling the weight of what he was saying. All around me, I could hear the piercing screams of frightened passengers. I glanced at Simon and took a deep breath, trying to erase the images my mind had created. It didn't work.

Simon shot me a frantic are-you-ready-to-land-this-thing? look, and then abruptly dropped the charade. My face must have given me away again.

"*Jeez*, Talia, I'm just messing around!" Jumping up, he stood there, awkward and apologetic. The imaginary airplane faded around him, turning back into the empty wreck. But it had been too real. I felt sick, like I needed to throw up. I took a few deep breaths, frustrated with myself.

"Sorry—I just, I don't know. It's just sad and terrible. Or something."

Sitting down on the edge of the plane's open cockpit, I

let my feet dangle and breathed in the cold arctic air. Since Mom's funeral, I couldn't bear to think about death. Pretending it was a game was even worse. If you've never seen the face of someone you love, all cold and quiet, and *gone*, then it's a little hard to explain.

"No one died, you know—in the crash," the Guitar Boy said as he sat down beside me. "There were only three crew members, the pilot and two others. Two of the men were hurt, but they recovered just fine."

I just nodded and looked out over the landscape. Rolling tundra scattered with glacial rock and scrub pine stretched into the distance before sinking toward the white frozen surface of Hudson Bay.

"Sorry—" I began, but he cut me off.

"Nah, it's all right." The Guitar Boy grinned, and then because he seemed more comfortable using other people's words to say what he meant, he pulled his guitar around and broke into song.

Up till now, Simon had only sung one song I knew. I'd only just met him and I'd already lost track of the number of songs he'd played today, spontaneously pulling his guitar around from where it hung across his back and bursting into song. But now as he began strumming, I recognized the melody as something Mom used to sing along to on the radio, and the force of it was so heavy and sudden I almost clapped my hands over my ears. If this song had come waltzing out of the speakers, I would have turned the radio off. Instead I took a deep breath and clenched my hands together in my lap. Though I didn't really want to, I forced myself to listen as that song floated out into the crisp morning air.

Surprisingly, it didn't make my chest ache like I thought it would. This boy and his guitar were different. I might have even gone on listening and actually liking it, but he didn't get very far into the song before a sudden *twang* interrupted him.

"Oh *man*." He fingered the long string that dangled, broken, from the neck of his guitar. "I hate it when perfectly good things break, ya know?"

"Yeah." I *did* know.

"Oh well." He shrugged. "Sometimes broken things are better for other stuff."

Loosening the key, he unwound the broken string, took my hand, and wrapped it around my wrist, twisting and securing it into a bracelet. I stared at it for a minute before glancing up at him.

"Thanks, Simon." I tried out his name, feeling self-conscious as I fingered the broken guitar string.

He smiled and slung his guitar over his shoulder again, twisting it around till it hung across his back. Then Simon jumped down onto the wing of the plane, and waited, humming, while I scrambled down after him.

Distractions

THAT FIRST WEEK without Dad dragged on, though the Guitar Boy and the Birdman made things seem a little less bleak. Long days never seem quite so long when there are interesting people in them, and my new friends were definitely interesting. Still, I needed to keep track of my days.

Dad had taken his pocket calendar with him and I didn't have one of my own. So instead, I made a paper chain, one loop of paper linked through another, and I strung it around the corners of my window alcove. I'd tear one loop off every day until he came back. That way I'd be able to count down the days until Dad returned, and I could forget how many he had been gone. I didn't know the exact day Dad would be back, but he expected the ice to go out the first week in July. So I gave him till July seventh. That morning, June fifth, I tore the eighth loop from my chain, leaving, hopefully, only thirty-two loops until Dad came back.

I should have been used to Dad being gone. He'd been away for a lot of my life. But I missed him. I missed the idea of him and all that that meant. Home. Mom. So when Sura invited Simon and his grandfather for dinner that eighth-loop night, at first I thought she was just trying to make me feel better. But as I watched the three of them around the table—Sura, Simon, and the Birdman—I realized they would have been here whether I was part of the mix or not.

The Birdman had been coming to Churchill for years. Fifteen to be exact, and he and Sura had been friends for most of that time. Simon had started coming with his grandfather a couple years ago.

"Mom is big on real-life education," Simon told me over a game of rummy later that evening. "I'm homeschooled, you know."

I looked up. "You're homeschooled?"

He nodded.

This surprised me. The homeschooled kids I knew were super smart, but kinda quiet. Simon was smart, but he was the furthest thing from quiet I'd ever met.

"Yep, I've been at home since second grade. Anyway, Mom and Dad are always trying to make sure I get a lot of real-life learning. And real-life environmental and cultural science experiences are sorta hard to come by when you're moving around a lot. My dad's in the military."

Simon laid down a red six, playing off the run I'd laid down on my last turn.

"I'm not about to argue spending the summers with my granddad in Churchill. Pretty sure it's the best real-life education I'll ever get." He grinned, and I glanced over at the Birdman, deep in conversation with Sura.

What would it be like to have someone like him for a grandfather? I didn't have any grandparents left, and what little I remembered of them had more to do with nursing homes than bird-watching and arctic adventure.

"Your turn," Simon said.

Smiling, I carefully laid down a run of spades and two kings, emptying my hand.

"I win." I leaned back in my chair and folded my arms across my chest.

Simon ran his hands through his hair until it stuck up on just one side.

"You're either really good at cards or really lucky," he said. This was the third time in a row he'd lost.

"My mom and I used to play a lot." I bit my lip. I hadn't meant to say anything about her. "And I—I guess I'm lucky." I fumbled over the words. I didn't want to leave anything about Mom hanging out there in space like an unanswered question. Simon would ask me about her, I knew he would, so I waited. But he never did. He just shrugged and gathered up the cards.

"Well, I think I'd better steer clear of you when it comes to card games," he said. "Not sure I can take losing like this every time."

"I guess I could let you win sometimes," I shrugged, relieved. "Maybe."

He laughed. "Wow. Maybe? That's super generous."

And it was my turn to laugh.

"Well, I have to be good at something!" I nodded at his guitar. "You've already got the music scene covered."

"Fair enough," he said, grinning. Then he pulled his guitar from where it hung on the back of his chair and broke into song. He made it look as easy as breathing.

We sang and played card games late into the night. And from that evening on, Simon and I spent almost every waking minute together. We did a lot of exploring and some bird-watching with Simon's grandfather, too. Even Sura came along a couple times, which was actually kind of nice.

Sura and I hadn't really talked about things since Dad left— about Mom, or even about how Dad was this sort of present-yet-absent force in my life. We didn't need to. Sura just seemed good at understanding. Or maybe she and Dad had talked before we came, so she knew about some of our brokenness. But if Dad had said anything to Sura, she never mentioned it. And I never asked.

Before Dad left, I'd been worried that Sura was all determined to be some kind of fill-in mom. But the better I got to know her, the more I realized that Sura wasn't actually treating me any different than she treated everyone else. She took care of people, loving them with the food she made and other things she did for them. Like when Dad came back from his first scouting trip on the ice. The special dinner Sura had made for us that night gave me a pretty good idea about what she thought of us. And on top of that she just sort of mothered everyone. Sura was one of those people who seemed to know what others need and wanted to do something about it. Once I figured this out, it didn't bother me quite so much. I wouldn't say we were best friends or anything, but I felt like we were starting to understand each other.

It was surprising. I didn't expect to like Sura very much— to like being around her. I'd been so sure that spending my summer with a stranger would be one of the worst parts of this whole thing. Maybe I'd been wrong about that.

When I wasn't with Sura or out exploring with Simon and the Birdman, I studied my wishes and waited anxiously by the radio receiver. Dad was good about calling in on the days we'd agreed upon. And every time the receiver crackled to life, my heart jumped into my throat, and relief would race clear to the ends of my fingers. Our conversations were always the same.

"VE4 portable W1APL, this is Dad. Over."

"Go ahead, W1APL." I'd say this into the radio. Then Dad would give me his location and I'd pull out the coordinate ruler. Lining it up with the grid marks on the map that hung over my desk, I'd make a mark where the latitude and longitude coordinates intersected, just like he'd shown me. With each new mark I made, I drew a line from the last location Dad had given me, charting his course across the wall. It was like playing connect-the-dots, only I couldn't tell what sort of picture would emerge from all of those connected lines. Maybe it would be a picture of the one thing we were both looking for and couldn't seem to find.

"How's the weather down south?" Dad would ask, his voice crackling over the radio static. I'd laugh and tell him I was wearing my sundress and flip-flops, which of course I wasn't. I couldn't even imagine myself in a sundress. I couldn't make that picture fit in this place of snow and ice, no matter what the sun might eventually do to warm things up.

"All is well on the ice," Dad would say. "No fish, but I'm not starving yet," which meant that he still hadn't seen any whales, but that he wasn't giving up.

"All is well on land, too," I'd tell him. "No bears and the

natives are friendly," which meant that I was safe and that Sura and I were doing okay.

"See you soon," Dad would finish, and we would say good-bye until our next scheduled call-in.

"Copy," I'd reply. "Over and out."

"Over and out," he'd respond.

And then the radio would go silent again.

The Stretch of Distance

ONE AFTERNOON WHEN THE SUN felt a little warmer than we were used to, the Birdman, Simon, and I packed a lunch and went looking for birds. It was weird, going to look for them when they were all around us. But apparently, big things would start happening in the bird world as the weather shifted toward spring.

"We are not looking for everyday, ordinary birds," the Birdman said. "We are looking for something else." The Birdman was pretty energetic for an old man, and sometimes his birding treks across Churchill got kind of intense. "We are looking for something that must be *sought*." And he swept his arms up and around, taking in all of Churchill and Hudson Bay.

"Sought?" I asked, wondering what, exactly, would be required.

"Sought," he repeated. "Do you think wonderful things will simply fall into your lap without the slightest effort on your part?"

I blinked at him. I'd never really thought about that before.

The Birdman wagged a teasing finger at me. "You of all people should know better, Talia Lea McQuinn," he said.

"I should?"

"You should," he insisted. "All good things always require a little effort."

I was beginning to turn this thought over in my mind when the Birdman turned to Simon. "We will have to keep our eyes open and our lips still."

Simon's lips were never still, and I laughed as he broke into spontaneous song—a made-up tune about people who talk too much and people who don't talk enough.

For the most part, though, we kept our mouths quiet and saw a number of birds that afternoon. None of them were all that unusual to the Birdman—he had a pretty exhaustive list. But for me, they were all rare and wonderful.

I wanted to learn to identify them, so the Birdman had given me his little pocket field guide to Canadian birds, and I pored over it, trying to memorize the names of the birds I'd never seen. Verdins and nuthatches, plovers and turnstones, gulls, ravens, and all kinds of birds of prey. There were photos and descriptions of songbirds, too—warblers, swifts, sparrows, larks—and other insect-eating birds. But none of those had arrived in Churchill yet. Things hadn't thawed out enough to hatch their breakfast, lunch, and dinner—mosquitoes, blackflies, and other pesky bugs. But they'd be on their way before long. Or so the Birdman said. Even though it had warmed up a bit, I had a hard time believing spring was only a few weeks away, considering how wintery everything still looked.

"Just wait," the Birdman said. "One morning you'll wake up and realize exactly how quiet it's been. There'll be songbirds everywhere, and you'll suddenly discover you've missed their song."

I figured he was right. He'd been coming to Churchill long enough, so I started listening for them—for those birds whose names I was just learning. And even though it was the first time I'd ever missed them, their absence suddenly felt loud.

Just before we stopped for lunch that afternoon, the Birdman led us out toward the end of a rocky peninsula jutting into the bay. The ice was beginning to recede from its edges, and I followed the Birdman's finger as he pointed out the shape of a massive bird in flight. Settled on a driftwood log bleached white by the sun and smooth as bone was an eagle majestically folding up his impressive wingspan. He studied us imperviously from where he rested on the tip of the peninsula.

The bald eagle was one of the few birds I could identify

without Simon or the Birdman's help. I'd seen them a few times before, and they never failed to make me catch my breath. They seemed to carry themselves differently than other birds, like royalty, even though they were scavengers.

"All right, you two," the Birdman said to Simon and me. "Tell me what you know about your national bird."

I laughed, because though we were in Canada, there was still a bit of national pride invoked by the Birdman's request, and Simon and I were happy to prove our allegiance.

"Well, it's a bird of prey, but it rarely kills its own food like hawks or owls do," Simon began. "Except for fish—it kills a lot of those. Mostly, it just eats whatever it can find."

"And it typically lives near large bodies of water and forests of old growth, because it likes to nest in tall trees," I said, scanning the snowy shoreline behind me. This far north the trees didn't get very big because of the poor climate conditions.

The Birdman nodded and followed my gaze.

"You're right," he said. "But if large old trees are unavailable, the eagle will nest on the ground. They're resourceful birds," he said.

"Oh, and they usually return to the same nest every year," I added, proud of what information I remembered from school.

"In 1782, the United States Seal was designed with the bald eagle on it," Simon said. "It has thirteen arrows in one talon and a thirteen-leafed olive branch in the other—for times of peace and times of war. Thirteen on account of the thirteen original colonies," he finished.

"How do you know that?" I asked.

Simon grinned and shrugged. "I like history."

"You *like* history?" I asked. "No one likes history."

Simon just laughed.

The Birdman handed me his binoculars and I peered through them, loving their magic. As I looked at the world through them, space opened up on itself, compressing everything around me. Where only a blur of feathers or a flash of color was visible before, the flicker of the eagle's opaque eyelid and the individual shafts of his wingtip feathers came into view—close and immediate. How nice it would be to see like that all the time—never missing the most important things, however tiny or far away. I shifted the binoculars away from the eagle and worked my way down the shoreline. But everything was empty and still. As far as I could tell, the eagle was alone.

"Oh, I almost forgot," I said suddenly, lowering the binoculars and returning them to the Birdman. "They mate for life."

The magnificent bird stretched his wings and stood on tiptoe for a minute, like he was assessing the wind, and then he lurched into the air. Simon and the Birdman watched him leave, but I scanned the sky and the shoreline for something else, wondering if his mate was out there somewhere. Wondering if he was going to her.

After we had done enough seeking to satisfy the Birdman, we ate the lunch Sura had packed for us: caribou jerky, fried touton, and a couple of apples with cheese. Then we washed it all down with water from our canteens.

I had watched Sura make touton one afternoon, perched on the counter as she deftly blended flour, baking powder, salt, bear fat, and water, using her hands to shape and knead the mixture into a smooth dough. The bear fat part made me nervous, but really, it was pretty much just like the fat my mom drained off bacon from those Saturday morning breakfasts we used to have together. Smelled the same, too. And with some sugar sprinkled on top, I might as well have been eating a doughnut from the corner bakery back in Woods Hole. I was getting brave about trying new things. Well, at least a little bit. It helped that Sura was sort of easing me into it.

After lunch, the three of us continued on, taking the back roads on the edge of town, wandering into the scrub now and then, though never very far because of the possibility of bears, and the Birdman refused to carry a gun.

Before long my boots were caked in icy mud from the road and peat moss from the scrub, and Simon was pulling lichen and twigs from my hair. I felt like a walking collection of arctic habitat.

"You look like you grew here," Simon said. "Like you belong here." He carefully untangled a bit of black spruce from my hair. His words hung in the air for a minute like a bird in flight. And then I let them land on me and sink in.

"Thanks," I said. And I ducked my head, hurrying after the Birdman before Simon had a chance to say any other nice things to me.

We made our way back toward the bay, which was still frozen over, but the sun had started warming the shallow waters, especially where the Churchill River emptied into the bay. Ice was gradually receding from shore and there was a good twenty yards of open water around the edge now. Even though it was early, we searched for shorebirds and waders with their long beaks and stilt-like legs. But our efforts went unrewarded; it was still too cold. Instead I listened as the Birdman described them, imitating their calls as he showed me their pictures in the field guide.

"In a few weeks' time sandpipers, plovers, and stints will scour this shoreline for food," he said. And my imagination was filled with flurries of wings and peeping cries that would ring out among the rocks and ripples.

We headed home after that, but before we got very far the Birdman suddenly stopped and pointed to the sky where a small white bird hovered, beating the air with his wings the way a hummingbird does. It looked almost as if there were an invisible string suspending him over the ring of open water around the shore.

"What is it?" I asked.

"It's an arctic tern," said the Birdman. "And he's early. That, my dear, is the bravest, most determined little bird to rise over icy waters."

"Why?" I asked. "Because he's so early?"

The Birdman nodded. "He's unusually early."

The bird hung against the blue spring sky, so white he looked more like the absence of blue in the shape of a bird. Only a small cap of dark plumage gave him away, low over his face, making him look like a tiny aviation pilot, his hat resting low on the bridge of his nose.

"He's brave because of the distance he covers," the Birdman continued. "The arctic tern makes a round-trip flight of about forty-four thousand miles every year. He flies from the Arctic pole to the Antarctic pole, and then back again, every year. It's the longest migratory distance of any bird on the planet. In his lifetime that little bird will make the equivalent of three round-trips to the moon!"

"Really? That's crazy!" Simon glanced up at the sky like he could somehow eyeball the distance across the blue cloudless span. It was hard to imagine one little bird covering that much ground. It made the distance I'd traveled from Woods Hole to Churchill seem like hardly anything at all.

Later that night, I dug out the coordinate ruler I used to plot Dad's route over the ice, and I measured the miles between

Woods Hole, Massachusetts, and Churchill, Manitoba. I drew a straight line across the map—the way the tern flies—adding it to the dot-to-dot picture slowly forming across the grid. Marking out the miles, I divided the distance the tern flew by the number of miles between Woods Hole and Churchill and came up with just over twenty-eight.

That little aviator bird flew the same distance between Woods Hole and Churchill *twenty-eight times* every year. I let out a low whistle. I'd only made the trip once, and that was more than enough for me. Compared to that little bird, I wasn't very brave.

I returned my ruler and pencil to their places in the desk drawer, then stood back and studied the map on the wall, trying to make a picture or a shape out of my dots and lines. But all I could see were two separate routes, and they wouldn't intersect until Dad came back for me.

Uncharted

THERE WERE TWENTY-FIVE paper loops left on my chain the afternoon the Birdman took Simon and me over to the CNSC. It was just over fourteen miles out of town, so we drove there in the Birdman's ancient Land Rover.

I told Simon I'd show him where my dad worked, though it would have been better if Dad were here so he could show him some of the stuff he was working on himself. Even then it wouldn't be half as interesting as Miss Piggy. But Simon wanted to go. I invited Sura to come along because it seemed like the right thing to do. But she shook her head, saying something about there not being enough room in the Birdman's truck, and the ride being a bit too bumpy.

The CNSC is a research facility for scientists, sort of like a small university right on the edge of the Arctic. Dad had been coming here for a while, so he was pretty good friends with a lot of the people who worked here year-round. The Birdman, too, had done some work at the CNSC—on birds of course—so he already knew his way around.

"Why don't you two go on in," he said as we pulled into the parking lot. "I'll come find you in a bit. And stay out of trouble." He pointed at Simon as we got out. Simon placed one hand over his heart in mock disbelief, and I laughed.

The research center had enough room for more than eighty people to come and stay, plus labs, office space, classrooms, a kitchen, laundry room, and dining hall. I gave Simon a quick tour before we wandered down to my dad's office.

I unlocked the door with the key Dad had given me before he left and flipped on the lights. It was strange. It looked like Dad had just stepped out for a minute. Papers and manila filing folders were piled everywhere, several crates of research equipment he hadn't needed were stacked in one corner, and various maps were pinned to all four walls, starred and dated where whales had been located in previous years. The place was a mess. Dad called it organized chaos, and he knew right where everything was, so I didn't dare touch anything for fear of misplacing something important.

"This is it," I said. "This is where you can almost always find my dad when he's not out on the ice." I gave the room a little one-handed sweep, wanting to apologize for the mess, but Simon didn't seem to care.

"This is really cool!" he said, eyeing the crates of equipment.

"My dad is a financial adviser for the military. I bet this is a lot more interesting! Where is he right now, your dad? Do you know?"

Simon stood in front of one of the maps on the wall.

"Hudson Strait, sixty-one degrees, thirty-two minutes north, and seventy-one degrees, forty-one minutes west," I said, tapping the spot on the map with my finger.

"What?" He looked at me like I'd just said something in a different language.

"Those are the coordinates," I said. "I chart Dad's location on a map I have at home every time he calls in. That's where he was the last time we talked. It helps me keep track of where he's at and where he's been. It's sort of nice to know, ya know?"

"But how do you know how to do that? To chart coordinates?"

"Dad taught me," I said, smiling. "Here, I'll show you."

I opened a cupboard door, revealing even more stacks of papers, boxes of notes, and a number of cardboard tubes. I grabbed one, uncapped it, and pulled out a map, unrolling it across the floor.

"See these?" I asked Simon. Thin lines ran at regular intervals from north to south on the right side of the map and from east to west along the bottom edge. "These are the meridian lines," I told him, tracing a line from top to bottom. "And these are the parallel lines." I ran my finger left to right. "They always stay the same even when maps are drawn in different sizes."

Simon nodded.

"So, picture a globe in your mind," I said. "Where's the equatorial line?"

"Right in the middle," Simon said easily.

"Good." I held up a ruler. "When plotting a location you always measure in minutes and seconds," I said. "That's what this ruler is marked with, rather than inches and centimeters."

Simon's face was a mixture of confusion and surprise. "Why would you measure distance in increments of time?"

"On a map, time and space are the same thing," I said. "We're just only used to thinking about time on the face of a clock. But if you think about time across the globe, you're actually covering a certain amount of distance every second. Time is just how fast the earth spins."

"All right," he said. But the puzzled look on his face gave him away.

"It's like this," I said, trying to explain it to Simon as Dad had explained it to me. "A sphere is three hundred sixty degrees around, right?"

Simon nodded.

"And there are three hundred sixty meridian lines on a map," I continued. "So, if you divide the total degrees of a globe into equal slices, you get one degree of space for each slice. Make sense?"

"Kind of," Simon said, but his furrowed brow didn't relax.

"Stay with me," I said. "Each one of those three hundred

sixty single-degree slices is the same as sixty nautical miles, and also sixty minutes of arc—or how round that distance is."

I showed him what I meant, curving my hands around an imaginary globe. "So, that's how you get measurements in distance, hours, minutes, and seconds. Each single-degree slice is sixty minutes wide. And there are sixty seconds in every minute. You just break down the measurements from there."

"Hmm," Simon said, running his hand through his hair until it stuck up off just one side.

"It's sort of like a card game," I said. "It makes more sense once you actually do it."

I handed Simon the ruler. The map we had spread out on the floor in front of us charted the Hudson Bay area, up into the Baffin inlets, and east toward Victoria Island. I pointed to the bottom edge of the map. "Churchill lies fifty-eight degrees, forty-six minutes, and nine seconds north of the equator," I said, "and ninety-four degrees, ten minutes, and nine seconds west of the prime meridian." I pressed my finger to the dot that marked Churchill on the map. "Here." I handed Simon the ruler. "Measure it and see if I got it right," I said.

Simon took the ruler, measuring against the parallel lines and counting up, until he came to Churchill's dot.

"Fifty-eight degrees, forty-six minutes, and nine seconds," he said.

"Great! That's the latitude," I said. "Now the longitude. It's a little trickier."

"Trickier?" Simon asked. "Don't you just do it the same way you did the latitude?" He moved the ruler until it lay parallel against the map. But unlike the latitude measurement, the lines didn't match up.

"See," I said, pointing to the ruler. "It's too long this way."

Simon tilted the ruler, already a step ahead of my explanation, slanting it until the lines matched up.

"Exactly!" I said.

"So on a globe, the meridian lines move closer together the farther you get from the equator. They move until they all meet at the poles, right?" Simon reasoned.

"Right."

"But on a map," Simon continued, "everything's flattened out, so you have to measure longitude at an angle."

Placing the ruler on a slant, Simon tallied up the minutes and seconds. "Ninety-four degrees, ten minutes, and nine seconds," he said.

I rocked back on my heels, beaming. "Good job! Now you can navigate your way anywhere in the world and always know exactly where you are."

Simon sat cross-legged beside me, fiddling with the coordinate ruler.

"You're a surprising person, Talia Lea McQuinn," he said.

I frowned, suddenly nervous.

He laughed. "I mean that in a good way. Like, you're different from other girls I know."

I didn't know what to say, and I felt my face heating up.

"You mean, because I can chart coordinates?" I shrugged. "It's not really that interesting."

"*No,* not just because you can chart coordinates. Other things, too," he said. "And it actually *is* interesting. To me." He handed me the ruler.

"Well, good," I said, my stomach flipping around. "Thanks."

But what I wanted to say was, *"You're a surprising person, too, Simon. And different than any other boys I know. Different than any other people I know, actually. And I like being around you. You make me feel brave, somehow."*

But I didn't say any of that. I just smiled and carefully put Dad's map away, thinking the words at Simon, and wishing I was brave enough to say them.

I turned off the lights in Dad's office, making sure everything was exactly the way I'd found it, and locked the door behind us. We hadn't gone more than a few steps down the hall when I heard the Birdman's voice. Simon grinned.

"He can't get very far without talking birds—" but I shook my head and held up my hand, cutting Simon off. The Birdman wasn't talking birds. We both paused in the hall, listening.

"So you're not concerned? It's going out early this year—I can almost guarantee it," a man said. I didn't recognize his voice.

"I wasn't aware you were in the business of guarantees, Kurt."

The Birdman's words were light, but there was an edge to his voice. It was that edge that made me stop. I held my breath. My heart was suddenly racing. We were eavesdropping, and I knew we shouldn't, but now I was too curious to stop. Simon looked at me and raised an eyebrow.

"Well, maybe not," Kurt said. "But you have to admit, McQuinn's pretty driven. Don't you think? Word around here is that when it goes, it'll go fast, and no one—no matter who he is or how much time he's spent out there—will get kind treatment from an iceberg. Not sure a man's life is worth those whales."

"He's a researcher, not a fool," the Birdman said. "And whether or not the ice goes out early, he's not going to take any more risks than he needs to. He's got Talia back here in Churchill."

"I hope you're right," he said. "And McQuinn will be the one we're all applauding if he comes back off the ice with word of those missing belugas."

"Yes, we will."

Simon and I stood quietly in the hall until the sound of the two men's voices receded down the corridor. But

I wanted to chase after them. I didn't care if they knew I'd been eavesdropping. I wanted to hear the rest of their conversation. I wanted to tell them *when*—not *if*. *When* my dad came back off the ice with news of the whales.

As Simon and I made our way through the corridors, I couldn't forget what I'd overheard. Everything had gone from good to horrible. One minute Simon and I were kneeling on the floor, charting our way across the Arctic, and the next minute the ice was coming off early and my dad was in danger. Even if Kurt wasn't in the business of guarantees, his words had settled and spread within me like cracks across the ice. My dad was out there. And no matter what the Birdman said, I wasn't so sure I was reason enough for Dad *not* to take any more risks than necessary.

After we finished at the CNSC, the Birdman drove us back to Churchill. He never said a word about his conversation with Kurt or anything about my dad at all, and I almost asked him if anyone at the CNSC had heard from him—just to see what he would say. But I was already scared, and talking about the danger my dad could be in wasn't going to help me feel any better. So I didn't say anything. And neither did Simon.

"Well, I think we've expended enough effort today to require nourishment!" the Birdman proclaimed. "How about some ice cream?" And without waiting for a response, he pulled up to the confectionery in town.

The Birdman's truck had jostled us over every pothole in the road on our way back, and I was actually feeling a little sick to my stomach. Though I wasn't sure if it was because of the ride itself, or the worry Kurt's words had flung over me.

"One cannot go this long without sustenance." The Birdman glanced at me in the rearview mirror and I tried to smile—tried to play along. Simon, of course, had no trouble, and he nodded, his face completely serious.

The Tamarack Confectionary had the best ice cream in Churchill, and we were all hungry. It definitely wasn't ice cream weather, but we walked around town anyway, eating our cones and watching tourists. The Birdman stopped and talked with a few people along the way. He was known in Churchill as the resident bird expert, and it was fun to hear him talk about birds with people who understood them. He reminded me a bit of Dad, always so excited by his life's work.

As we walked around, I couldn't help but worry if Dad was okay. The last time he called in, there had been thirty paper loops left on my paper chain, but he still hadn't found his whales, and I could tell by the sound of his voice he was concerned. He was a man of science. He believed every effect had a cause. But this time, the effect was so great and the cause so mysterious, I was beginning to worry he wouldn't ever have his questions answered.

Sura believed mysterious things sometimes happened just

because they *did*, and that whether or not we ever understood why didn't matter as much as what we did with the mystery. "There's beauty in not having all the answers," she'd said recently. "It makes your heart grow."

But I wasn't so sure. Sura's words and thoughts of Dad swirled around in my brain as the Birdman, Simon, and I made our way back home.

I couldn't help but wonder: You can chart distance across a map in minutes and seconds. This I knew. But could you chart the growth of your heart by the things you do and say, by what you think and how you feel? One gave you a physical location in the world. Maybe the other could give you answers to impossible questions.

I was so lost in thought that when Guns N' Roses started crooning "Don't Cry" over the radio, I reached across the backseat and flipped it off like I usually did when one of the songs Mom used to sing came on. I didn't even think twice about it. But Simon didn't get it, so he reached across the seat and flipped it back on.

I sat stiff and quiet for a few seconds, then reached over and turned the radio off again. I felt the Birdman's eyes on me in the rearview mirror, but I didn't look at him. The silence in the cab was thick enough to drown in, and from across the front seat, Simon turned the dial on again, and the words came flooding back into the silence.

Angry now, I reached for the dial a third time, but Simon

grabbed my hand and held it. Jerking away, I was all ready to say something cliché about silence being golden once in a while, but the look on his face made me bite back my words. He wasn't teasing me or messing around. He was serious. Confused.

"Why'd you do that?" he asked.

I bit my lip and looked away, out the window.

"*Hey*. Why did you do that?" Simon leaned over so he could see my face.

So much for letting it go.

I shrugged. "I don't feel like listening to the radio."

"Why not?"

I shrugged again.

"Don't you like music?" His voice fell, and I suddenly thought of his guitar and his songs.

"No—no, Simon. I do like music. I do. Really. It's just that—" I stopped. I didn't know how to explain without telling him about Mom, and I didn't want to talk about her. I didn't want him to feel sorry for me or anything. "I just don't like some songs, is all," I said. But I knew this wasn't going to be enough of an answer for Simon.

His face twisted into a frown and he slumped back against the seat.

"Why do you play the guitar and sing so much?" I asked.

Simon stared at me, skeptical, like he thought it was a trick question.

"Because," he said. It was so simple for him. "You can

say things through songs you can't say any other way. And people listen. Songs get inside you and kind of stay there. They remind you of different things. Memories. People." He shrugged.

"That's just it," I said. "Some songs remind me of things I don't want to think about."

Even though she wasn't there to sing along, I could still hear my mom's voice in my head. And when the song ended, I would have to jump right back into the silence her absence had created. Sometimes it was easier not to listen in the first place.

"You know, old songs can start to remind you of new things," Simon said, "if you let them. Maybe you should listen again. You might be surprised." He held my gaze until I looked away.

And through it all, the Birdman never said a word.

Birthday Wish

I'D KNOWN DAD WOULD BE out on the ice for my birthday, and I'd been telling myself for the last few days it was okay. It was fine. But the truth was, it wasn't fine at all. He was missing this. And it's not like it was ever going to happen again—my turning thirteen. I wanted him here.

Since he was gone, and there was nothing I could do to change that, I decided to pretend it was just another ordinary day. I hadn't said anything to Sura, or to Simon and the Birdman, because it seems sort of weird to go around telling people it's your birthday, like you need them to congratulate you. I didn't want anyone to feel like they had to give me gifts or anything. Besides, I'd been born on June thirteenth, and turning thirteen on the thirteenth wasn't something I wanted to bring a lot of attention to.

It's surprising how many people actually believe thirteen is unlucky.

But I definitely couldn't control my birthday, and I simply could not afford to be afraid or superstitious about my own age for an entire year. So, when I woke up on the morning of June thirteenth, I opened my eyes and whispered to myself, "Happy golden birthday, Tal. You're thirteen today. Congratulations." Just like Mom would have. Then I got up, got dressed, brushed my teeth, and headed downstairs for breakfast. But before I even got to the landing, I knew something was up.

There were balloons pinned to the railing—thirteen of them. I came down the stairs slowly, batting each one on my way.

At the bottom of the stairs stood Sura, Simon, and the Birdman, waiting to greet me.

"Happy birthday!" the Birdman exclaimed, and Simon burst into a rousing rendition of the song. When he finished I clapped. Then I bowed from where I was on the stairs, sticking one hand out behind me, as Simon had done the first day I saw him. And as I straightened up and looked around, all my words disappeared.

There were balloons pinned to the back of each kitchen chair. Streamers hung from the kitchen cabinets to the ceiling, draping low over the table so we'd have to duck under them. And Sura had made a huge chocolate cake that sat in the center of the table, decorated with thirteen pink candles.

It was those candles that did it. Those thirteen pink candles. I had to swallow hard a couple times before I was certain I could talk around the lump in my throat.

I hadn't breathed a word to anyone. Not a word! But I also hadn't considered that Sura might've already known all about my birthday. That Dad might have told her before he left. It was the only way she could have known. And that was the part that kept making me want to cry. He'd told her. Dad had *remembered*, and even though he couldn't be here himself, he'd made sure Sura understood my birthday was special.

"Thank you," I said, taking them in. I couldn't believe it—they were all dressed up. Sura was wearing a blue dress. Both Simon and the Birdman wore dress shirts and ties. The Birdman's mustache was curling up especially well today.

"You're all so fancy!" I said, laughing as Simon tugged at his shirt collar in mock discomfort.

"Yes," he said. "And I hope you appreciate it!"

"It's not every day you celebrate a golden birthday," the Birdman said, adjusting his tie though it was already perfect. "One has to mark these sorts of events with the appropriate attire, you know."

I nodded and glanced down. I was wearing jeans and a sweatshirt.

"Hang on a second," I said. "I'll be right back." I took the stairs two at a time up to my room.

I changed quickly and then stood in front of the mirror that hung against my closet door, studying my reflection for a minute. The last time I'd worn this dress I'd been a little shorter and a little flatter. It fit me differently now. *Better*, I decided. It fit me better.

Dad had helped me pick out this dress last fall for my school band program. Our neighbor had offered to take me shopping, but Dad had surprised me, insisting he take me himself. I think he was trying to fill that Mom-shaped space a little, because he'd never taken me shopping before. Once we were there, though, I knew the trip was a mistake. Everything reminded me of Mom, and that she should have been with me instead.

I was about to leave empty-handed, until I saw the dress I wore now—mossy green, simple. When I tried it on, Dad said something I would never forget. He told me I looked beautiful. Just like Mom.

And that sealed the deal.

As I came down the stairs now, I could tell my new friends were impressed.

"Well, look at you!" the Birdman exclaimed. He promptly offered me his arm, the way a gentleman would. I took it, laughing as he led the way to the table. He pulled my chair out for me, and then for Sura as well, before seating himself and throwing his arm comfortably around the back of Simon's chair.

Leaning across the table, Sura lit the candles on my cake

130

and then reached over and squeezed my hand. This time, I didn't pull away from her touch.

It was strange, but lately I felt like I was learning some new kind of skill. It was almost like learning to tie my shoes all over again, memorizing the complicated pattern of loops and crossovers until it was second nature. But this time, instead of my shoes, I was lacing up my heart. Or maybe my new friends were doing it for me.

Simon seemed a little quieter than usual, and other than his rousing rendition of "Happy Birthday," he kept his songs to himself for the rest of the morning. I wondered if he might still be upset about the car radio thing. Maybe he was being quiet because he figured I didn't want to hear his songs. Or *any* songs. But that wasn't the case at all.

While Sura and the Birdman took out plates and silverware, I scooted my chair closer to Simon's.

"Thanks for singing," I said.

He looked surprised. "It's all right then?" he asked, sounding relieved.

I nodded. "Of course it's all right. I love your songs."

Simon rested his foot on the bottom rung of my chair and grinned until he seemed entirely made up of that smile.

Then Sura lit the candles, and I knew exactly what came next.

"Make a good wish," the Birdman said.

I smiled, because no one needed to worry about that. I

was a champion wish-maker. So I closed my eyes and wished for the one thing all the rest of my wishes depended on, most especially my *big wish*.

It would be magic if today—my golden birthday—a unicorn came sailing into Hudson Bay. I knew the reality of that actually happening was about as unlikely as Miss Piggy suddenly taking flight, but that's what wishes are for. So that's what I wished as I blew out my candles. I wished for a narwhal whale. My unicorn.

And then we had chocolate cake for breakfast.

After I licked the last of the chocolate frosting from my fork, Simon and I decided to walk down to the shore. The Bird-man had mentioned something about seeing some new plovers and we wanted to see if we could catch a look at them.

When we reached the shore, I looked out over the flat stretch of ice, trying to imagine what it would look like to see a narwhal whale emerge from beneath the surface.

"So, what'd you wish for, Tal?" Simon asked suddenly, and he chucked a rock out over the bay. I watched as it landed with a satisfying *plunk*.

You're not supposed to tell wishes. Not birthday wishes. Not any wishes. Everyone knew that. Only secret wishes come true.

But Simon's question made me wonder if maybe I had it backward, because I was doing an awful lot of wishing in secret and not much was happening. Maybe there was more to it than just waiting and hoping. I knew you weren't supposed to share your wishes with the whole world, but maybe you did have to share them in some small way. Maybe they had to get out somehow before they could come true— like butterflies breaking out of their chrysalises. Maybe my wishes couldn't come true till I let them breathe. Opened the lid on my jar a little.

So I took a breath. "I wished for unicorns." The words came out slowly, like they were testing their wings.

"Unicorns?" Simon squinted at me, sort of disbelieving. "You made a birthday wish on unicorns?"

"Narwhals," I said, clarifying. "I wished for a narwhal whale."

He frowned and tossed another rock. It fell shy of his previous throw.

"Why are you wishing for narwhals?" He seemed a little disappointed, like he'd expected me to be wishing for something else.

"Because. Unicorns grant wishes."

I regretted saying something as soon as the words were out of my mouth. That's the trouble with talking, you can't un-say things. Up to this point I hadn't told anyone about my faith in the whales, not even Dad, and now it sounded stupid, floating through the air and out over the water. Especially now that I was thirteen.

"So, you're wishing for something that grants wishes?" Simon didn't look at me as he searched the ground for another smooth stone.

I stared at him, trying to see if he was making fun.

"Something like that," I said, and I threw a rock as hard as I could.

"What's up with you and wishing?" he asked.

I just shrugged and stared out at the bay.

On the inside, I was dying to race back to the blue house, drag my jar of wishes from beneath the bed, and empty its contents into Simon's lap. I wanted him to see them, and I'd never wanted anyone to see my wishes before—at least, no one except Mom. *There*, I'd say, shaking my wishes into his lap. *These are the reason I'm wishing for unicorns. These are the reason I can't sleep at night, the reason I still have hope, and actually, these are the reason I'm here at all. Because if my wishes can come true, then maybe I will finally get the chance to say good-bye to my mom.*

I needed to see her one last time—not in my imagination or my memory, but for real. I needed to touch her face, feel the ends of her hair, hug her hard. I wanted to tell her—to her real, alive, awake face—that I would give anything to have her back. That I missed her. That I would never forget her. Most of all, I wanted to tell her that I loved her.

But I didn't do any of those things. I didn't run back to the blue house to show Simon my jar, and I didn't say anything about my big wish. I didn't even really answer his question. But Simon didn't press it, and he didn't ask me anything else. He didn't try to make any lame jokes, and he didn't say I was crazy for wishing for a whale that grants wishes. Instead, he just sat there quietly and waited.

I fingered the smooth stones that lay all around us on the beach. It had taken hundreds of years for a glacier to drag them here, and then many more years for that melted glacier to wash them over sand and silt, and against other rocks until they were smooth and soft. Perfect, without any broken edges. Moraine.

I glanced up at Simon.

"My mom used to say that people make wishes because they want something bad enough to let everything else go—everything except that one thing they're hoping for."

Simon ran his hands over the rocks beside him, searching for the perfect stone. He didn't look at me and he didn't say anything. He didn't even ask me what I was hoping for—what I wanted badly enough to let everything else go.

I was beginning to think how dumb I must have sounded when Simon stood up. He held a rock between his fingers, almost completely flat and perfectly smooth.

"Did you know that you can make a wish on a skipped rock?" he asked.

"How do you skip a rock?"

"Like this," he said, and he arched his arm to the side,

the rock held flat between this thumb and forefinger, and threw it across the surface of the bay in that narrow space of open water between the shore and the ice. I watched as it skimmed the water, skipping once, twice, three times before disappearing beneath the surface. Simon smiled slowly and sat back down beside me.

"So, what did *you* wish for?" I asked.

"I wished for your unicorn," he said.

And at that moment I decided Simon might just be one of the best people I'd ever known. So for some crazy, un-explainable, *golden birthday* reason, I leaned over and kissed him. Then, I sprung up and headed for the blue house without a backward glance.

Gifts

ONCE I GOT BACK TO the house, I had to stand on the porch and catch my breath for a couple of minutes. I couldn't believe I'd actually kissed Simon, and I was suddenly terrified it might have been a mistake. But it was too late to take it back. Turns out that kissing is sort of like talking. You can't un-kiss anyone any more than you can un-say something. I'd never kissed anyone before—at least, not the sort of kiss you actually mean. It was probably best just not to think about it too much. The next time I saw Simon, I'd try and explain. Apologize, or something.

Later that night, after all the birthday festivities were over, Sura offered to make whatever I wanted for dinner because it was my birthday. Even though it was late and I was feeling more anxious to talk to Dad than hungry, I suddenly realized I didn't just want to sit there while Sura cooked for me. I wanted more than that. I wanted to give her something—do something for her, like she had been doing for me all along. Loving me with the things she made. I asked her if I could help.

I think it surprised her, but she quickly agreed, and together we made pizza with a touton crust. It wasn't like the pizza back home, but I had to admit, it was still pretty good. And cooking with Sura helped keep my mind off waiting for Dad's call.

Once we finished eating, Sura cleared the dishes and then returned to the table with a tiny wooden box in one hand. She slid it across to me and leaned back, watching.

"What's this?" I asked. It looked like a jewelry box, covered with intricate Inuit designs.

"It's your birthday gift," she said. "From your father."

"From Dad? Really?"

"You didn't think he would forget, did you Talia? Your father loves you—you must know this."

"I do, I—I just—" I shrugged. "I just didn't think he'd *plan* things."

But he had. And whatever leftover traces of bitterness I might have felt over his absence today slowly broke apart and floated away, leaving me with only hopeful expectation as I waited for Dad's voice to come crackling over the radio airwaves.

Dad had taken the time to tell Sura about my birthday, and he'd also taken the time to get me a gift, leaving it behind so I was sure to have it today. He could have waited and given it to me himself after he got back. Or he could have given it to me before he left, I guess. But he didn't. He made sure I had it today so I *knew* he remembered. It was important. *I* was important. Even though Mom was gone, and he was out on the ice, and absolutely everything was different, I still mattered.

I lifted the lid on the little wooden box. Inside was a pendant necklace with a delicate silver chain.

I laid it across my palm, cradling it like a living, breathing thing. The charm strung on the chain was no longer than the first knuckle of my little finger, and as white as bone, intricately carved and spiraling to its tiny pointed tip. I knew exactly what it was. I just couldn't get over the fact that Dad knew how much this would mean to me.

It was a tiny horn.

And not just any horn. A unicorn horn.

"It's made from the ivory of a narwhal tusk," Sura said.

I swallowed hard, the lump in my throat rising again. I'd been fighting it off a lot today.

I fumbled with the clasp for several seconds, my hands shaking, and then finally held it out to Sura for help. She lifted the hair off my neck and secured the clasp. I laid my hand over the charm, pressing its tiny weight against my chest.

How had he known?

"It's a good gift, then?" Sura was watching me, her head tilted to one side.

I nodded. "It's a good gift," I said, the words almost stuck in my throat. "Really good."

She smiled, and then slid something else across the table. A flat package wrapped in brown paper.

"From me," she said.

I blinked. I hadn't expected anything from Sura. She'd already thrown me a party and made me a cake. Now she was giving me a gift on top of all that.

"Thank you." I smiled across the table.

At first I thought it was a book. Maybe a field guide of my own. I'd been using the Birdman's *Field Guide to Canadian Birds* so often that the pages were starting to look even more ragged than when he'd first loaned it to me. But I couldn't have been more wrong.

It was a picture in a carved wooden frame. I pulled it free from the paper and studied the face of the girl in the photograph.

She was smiling—a dimple showing on only one side, same as me. Her nose was wrinkled like she thought whoever was taking the picture was being silly.

I glanced up at Sura. I didn't know what to say.

Sura's gift to me was a picture of my mom as a young woman, before I was ever born, maybe before she and Dad were married, and long, long before cancer. She was beautiful, and I pressed her cheek to my lips and kissed her, just like I did with my wishes every time I pulled them from their jar.

I studied my mom's face, remembering her nose and the shape of her eyes, the way her eyelashes curled up, and how the little hollow above her upper lip was shaped exactly like a tear. I placed my finger in the hollow above my own lip.

I'd never seen this picture before. The most amazing difference between this one and all the pictures I'd seen of my mom until now was her hair. It wasn't long like it was when I knew her. It was shorter, bobbed at her chin like I used to wear mine when I was younger. Almost exactly as she used to cut it for me.

In all of the other pictures I had of Mom, her hair was long, thick, and dark.

That's how I remembered her. Until she got sick.

I'd come home from school late one afternoon because I was working on an after-school English project. Mom made us peanut butter and honey sandwiches for dinner, without the crusts, and we curled up together in the library. It was much cozier than sitting at the kitchen table.

Mom was doing research and I was brushing out her hair. She let me do this sometimes, and I loved pulling a thick-handled brush until not a single strand was tangled. She looked like a queen.

"You know, Tal, the medicine I'm on is very strong," she said. "It might make me sick."

"Is it strong enough to kill the cancer?" I asked her.

She was quiet for a long time. "I hope so," she said. "It's going to try. But it's going to kill some good things, too."

"What kind of good things?" I asked. I was scared, because being sick is bad enough, but the thought that even the medicine would make her sick terrified me. That's not how it was supposed to work.

"It's going to make my hair fall out," she said.

I stopped mid-stroke as the weight of that brush grew impossibly heavy. I wanted to throw it out the window—through the glass. It wasn't fair. There were tears running down my face before I realized I was crying. But Mom didn't cry. She was brave.

"I'll tell you what," she said, turning around and cupping her hands around my face. "Let's not let the cancer or the chemotherapy take it."

I looked at her, unsure of what she meant. She reached over and pulled a pair of scissors from the drawer in her desk.

"Let's cut it," she said to me, and she smiled, wiping tears from my face as I stared at her in shock, trying to decide if she was serious.

She was.

"How about you cut it for me, Tal," she said. "Would you?" She placed the scissors in my hands.

I was eleven years old, but I knew she was telling me something important. She trusted me to do this for her. So I nodded, biting my lip as tears ran down my face.

Running my shaking hands through her hair, I lifted it from her neck and placed the open blade of the scissors against the strands.

"Here?" I asked. "This short?"

She shook her head. "Shorter."

I moved the blades up higher until they were just below her ears.

"There," she said. "Right there."

I closed the blades, again and again, until her hair, long and dark, lay all around us and covered the floor.

When I was finished, both our faces were wet with tears. Mom wrapped her arms around me, and we sat there, rocking back and forth on the floor as she kissed my face over and over again. She reached up to hold the ends of her hair, cropped short and choppy around her face as though she were saying good-bye to an old friend.

"I'm sorry, I'm sorry," I cried.

But she shook her head and held me tighter.

"Talia Lea," she said, "this is the most beautiful haircut I have ever had."

And I knew she was really saying she loved me.

When Dad came home later that evening, he stopped short when he saw Mom. His eyes got very wide, but he didn't say a word. He just reached out and ran his hand through her hair. And when his fingers met the cropped ends, he just cupped his hand against the back of her bare neck like it had always belonged there.

"Talia cut it for me," Mom said softly, wrapping her arms around me, sandwiching me between the two of them. "Isn't it beautiful?"

Dad smiled at down me, his eyes swimming.

"Nice job, Tal," he said to me. "You're beautiful."

The last part he said to her.

I clasped the picture to my chest and looked up at Sura.

"Thank you," I breathed. "Thank you so much."

Sura smiled. "You are so like her," she said. "And I don't mean just the way you look. You are like her here, too." And she pressed her hand over her heart. "She was only six years older than you are now." She nodded at the picture in my hands. "It was her first summer in Churchill and she was working as an intern at the CNSC. But rather than stay at the science center, she insisted on staying in town with someone who lived here. 'I want to be a part of the culture,' I can remember her saying. 'I want to live it, to breathe it, and taste it and hear it. And I can't do that if I'm away from everything.'"

"So she stayed with you?"

"Me and my mother." Sura nodded. "And she lived this place and our people. The Inuit. She breathed our air, and tasted our food, and listened to our language and our stories."

"My dad said you two were friends."

"Yes. Though not at first. We were very different. But before the summer was over, we were close. She promised to come back. And she did. She came back for two more summers before she met your father."

"And then I was born."

"I imagine so," Sura said, her eyes crinkling at the corners when she smiled. "I did not hear from your mother very much after that. But your father came back to Churchill many times, and he stayed with my mother and me as well. So you see, Talia, your family has been here for a long time."

I looked around the room. The kitchen with its brown linoleum floors and green cupboards. The front room, lit by the light of the fire in the big old wood stove and one lonely table lamp. It was a warm place. Friendly. Like it knew you might need to stay a while and warm up before you faced the frozen world outside the front door. I thought of how this house had kept my mom warm so many years ago.

I stared down at the face of the girl in the picture, soaking her up. Memorizing my mom's younger face. Her short hair. Her fearless eyes.

"Thank you, Sura," I said. "I think this might be the best birthday gift ever."

I glanced at the clock that hung on the kitchen wall, shocked to see it was already ten fifteen. My birthday was almost over and I still hadn't heard from Dad. His usual call-in time was eight P.M., but more than two hours had passed and the radio remained silent. It wasn't like him and we both knew it. Why hadn't he called? Had something happened? Had he forgotten?

Sura must have noticed the worried look on my face.

"I'm sure you'll hear from him soon, Talia," she said. "Maybe he had a long day and just fell asleep."

"Maybe," I said. But I wasn't so sure. I was about to head to bed when Sura stopped me.

"There is one last thing." Sura stood up, nodded toward the window. "Come outside with me," she said.

"Why?"

"Just come."

I pulled my coat from its hook and followed Sura out onto the porch. We were so far north—so far from the equator—that the closer we got to spring, the longer the daylight lasted. But the hours had ticked quietly by while we made dinner and sat at the table opening presents, and now darkness had drawn over everything like a heavy blanket.

Sura stood at the rail looking up into the night sky. At first I couldn't see anything because my eyes were used to the light of the kitchen. But after a minute they adjusted to the darkness and the sky came alive.

"It's like magic," I whispered, and Sura smiled.

"Of course," she said. "Churchill is magic. And it's putting on a show tonight. In honor of your birthday."

It was spring and the perpetual darkness of winter was fading into the light. But even so, the aurora borealis, the northern lights, danced like pale ghost flames above us. Red and green and white, they shivered and sashayed over the night sky. They began in a straight line across the horizon and stretched upward toward the highest point in the sky—that point where a globe would have spun on its axis. I knew a little about them from my science classes back home. Something about sun storms and the earth's magnetism. I couldn't remember it all, but even if I did, no scientific explanation could have prepared me for the light display that night over Churchill, Manitoba.

I stood staring up at the twilight sky, watching the patterns shift and change, and I was so lost in the beauty of it that I jumped when Sura broke the silence.

"The Inuit say that a great abyss lies at the edge of the world," she said. "A narrow way spans it, and those who have died are guided carefully across to a place of great rest." She paused. "There's no pain or disease there. Spirits guard the way across the abyss, guiding souls to paradise and lighting the way with brilliant torches." She smiled and looked up.

There was a quietness, a kind of deep-down stillness inside me as I watched the lights dance, backtracking, repeating themselves in indistinguishable patterns and shifting colors. They were so bright they actually cast a glow over the crusty, glazed snow.

As I stood there, I thought about Sura's story. Mom had said that people make up stories to help them explain things they can't believe, or to help them believe things they can't explain. To help them understand. And people dying is a pretty hard thing to understand. It made sense that the Inuit had their own story for this very thing.

An hour later, when Dad still hadn't called, I finally went to bed. I told myself that it was probably because he was on his way back. Why call when he would see me in just a few hours?

As I lay in bed, the aurora borealis dancing outside my window, I clutched the picture of my mom's young face against my chest, against the necklace Dad had given me. And I fell asleep like that, holding onto both of them for dear life.

Spring Winds

EVERY DAY NEW PEOPLE WERE arriving in Churchill, which was ironic because amid the dozens and dozens of new faces in town, the one face I kept looking for was still absent. I had hoped Dad would surprise me by returning early, even though it was unlikely, but he hadn't come home yet and he still hadn't called. Dad's absence was beginning to feel like a toothache—always there, always throbbing and making it difficult to think about anything else for very long. And I was beginning to get worried.

I tried to distract myself by spending time with Simon. When we weren't out bird-watching, we were people watching, and there was a lot to see. The tourists traveled by train or plane, and a few by boat. They came like they knew spring was only weeks away, eager to see the wildlife that would appear out of hiding as the snow melted. Eager for the promise of arctic adventure. They came to see the bears and to explore Churchill's history.

But mostly, people came for the whales. They came knowing of their absence. At least, some of them did. A few were surprised and disappointed, but no one was deterred. It was the talk of the town, Churchill's missing whales, and it created a contagious sense of mystery. Each morning people would line the shore along the bay's estuary and wait, searching the cloudy waters for white whales.

Simon thought the tourists were silly. They were so excited about the absence of the very thing they'd come to see. But I think I understood how they felt, how just the hope of something can pull at you. I felt sorry for them. And I felt sorry for myself, because I was waiting, too.

That morning, as I tore another paper loop from my chain, I realized there were only seventeen loops left. It was the twentieth of June. Dad had been gone for twenty-five days, and out on the bay, the ice was shifting from opaque white to steel gray. It was getting thin, tired of fighting against the growing warmth.

Back in Woods Hole it was summer. Here in Churchill, spring was still on its way, but it was coming so fast I was afraid I might actually miss it. In the north, spring is already right on top of you once the ice breaks apart, running massive chunks aground as the tide goes out. But just before the ice begins breaking up, fierce warm winds come rushing out of the south. It was a sure sign of change, that wind, and it would blow warm and fast, eating up the snow and ice.

The spring winds arrived just after my birthday, and the morning they came, I knew something was different even before I got out of bed. I could hear the wind racing around the blue house, rattling the windows and skittering over the shingles. And when an especially fierce gust buffeted against the house, the staircase would let out a funny kind of groan, like it was protesting all the exuberance outside. Everything felt all stirred up and it made me anxious, like I needed to dance around, and I'm not normally the twirling type.

When I was little, Dad used to hold tight to my wrists and spin me around until my feet flew off the ground. I'd get dizzy and all twirled up, inside and out. All I could see was my dad's laughing face and the world spinning away in a kind of breathless blur.

That's what it was like today as I sat with Simon. A happy, breathless blur.

It had been a week since I kissed him and neither of us had said anything about it. The more time that passed, the more I was afraid I'd ruined something. Maybe Simon hadn't wanted me to kiss him. He might even be mad about it.

I hadn't done it on purpose, exactly. It was just that he was so great, and there on the shore after he wished for unicorns for me, my mouth just took over and did the kissing before the rest of me had a chance to decide whether it was a good idea or not. So I thought I should apologize. Plus I felt a little nervous and shy about the whole thing.

"I'm sorry I kissed you," I told him.

"You're sorry?" He looked so disappointed I realized maybe he wasn't mad. Maybe I hadn't ruined anything after all.

"Well," I hesitated, "I guess I'm only sorry if you are."

Simon grinned, running a hand through his hair until it stuck up on just one side, the way I liked it.

"I'm not sorry," he said, still grinning. "You can kiss me anytime you like." And he looked like he might burst into song.

I felt so relieved, I sat down next to Simon, feet dangling off the edge of the porch. Beside me, Simon strummed his guitar, singing softly under his breath. I closed my eyes and leaned back, hands folded behind my head.

"This is nice," I said to no one in particular. It had been a long time since I felt this comfortable with someone. The only thing keeping it all from being completely great, keeping me from feeling completely at ease, was Dad. Every time I walked past the radio, I stopped and stared at it. At first I thought that maybe something was wrong with it. Maybe the battery had died or it was broken. Sura even asked someone from the CNSC to take a look at it. Just to be sure. But the radio was fine.

So I decided that Dad had probably just lost track of time. It had happened before. And it was probably hard to keep track of your days, pocket calendar or not, out on the open water. Or maybe Dad had finally found his little white whales, and in all the excitement he'd forgotten to call me. And because that was a much better alternative than any of the hundred terrible scenarios I'd imagined while lying awake at night, it seemed like a good idea to hang on to that one. Dad had found his whales. He'd forgotten to call. He'd be in off the ice in about two and a half weeks. Maybe less. And as long as I focused on that, and kept hanging out with Simon, things were okay. Easier.

Simon stopped playing and I opened my eyes, squinting up at him. He was staring at me kinda funny, and I pulled myself up on one elbow.

"What? What's wrong?"

"Nothing." Simon smiled and started strumming his guitar again. "I just thought you were sleeping and you looked pretty."

"You think I look pretty?"

"Sure." He kept strumming.

I stretched back out and smiled up at the sky, my insides swooping.

The screen door slammed behind us, caught by a gust of wind as Sura came out on the porch. She leaned over the rail beside Simon and me and stood there for several long minutes, smiling and taking in all of that warm spring wind. None of us said anything, we just looked out across the bay, quiet and windswept.

After a time, Sura spoke. "I love this weather." She sighed. "And this wind. It's like music. Different than winter wind. Softer. Have you heard of Inuit throat singing, Talia?" she asked, turning to me.

Her question seemed totally unrelated to the weather. I looked up at her, confused by the suddenness of it.

Simon quit playing his guitar and leaned back against the side of the house, his face expectant. "It's really cool," he said.

I watched Sura as she closed her eyes. She looked like she was listening for something. Maybe she was waiting for just the right moment—like Mom used to before she told a story.

After a few seconds of silence, Sura took a deep breath and broke into a low, eerie wailing sort of song. It was unlike anything I'd ever heard. Wild and rushing, like the wind. Part cry, part chant, she almost seemed to echo herself, repeating a single note and then instantly dropping to harmonize with herself. And with such fluidity that if I didn't know better, I'd think there were two women singing instead of just one. When she stopped, she took one look at my face and burst out laughing.

"Where did you learn how to do that?" I asked.

"My mother taught me," she said. "And her mother taught her, whose mother taught her, and on and on until at the very beginning, it was taught to us by the wind itself." Sura smiled. "It's a story of course, but it's beautiful, don't you think?"

It *was* a beautiful idea—that the wind could teach some-one to sing. And if any wind could do it, it would be this warm, twirled-up wind. Spring was coming. It really was.

I wanted to laugh and cry at the same time. Joy and relief. But I was afraid, too, because that meant the ice could come off the Bay at anytime. And no matter what excuses I made up for him, if the ice went out before Dad came back, noth-ing I told myself could protect him from danger.

Ice Out

TWELVE DAYS LATER, ON JULY second, the ice on Hudson Bay finally gave way, piling on shore as the wind drove it out of the water or pushed it out to sea.

There were just four loops left on my paper chain. Dad had been gone for six weeks.

The day after my birthday, Sura had called the CNSC and talked to one of the guys my dad worked with on occasion. We thought maybe he would have some news of ice conditions or updates and reports from Dad's team. But he hadn't heard a word.

"Nothing? Really?" I said when Sura got off the phone. Disappointment and now fear felt like an actual thing lodged in the back of my throat.

"Your dad took a full team with him, Talia," Sura said, her voice calm and steady. "He would really have no reason to call the CNSC or report any of his findings until he came back and had a chance to sort through all of the data they collected. And I'm sure there's a perfectly logical explanation he hasn't been able to call us, either. Perhaps the radio failed."

That made sense. After all, the Birdman had said that Dad wouldn't take any more risks than he needed to. And Dad knew I was here, waiting. But things that seemed so reasonable in my head didn't necessarily agree with the things in my heart. I wanted something real, something I could hold on to.

I lay in the darkness that night and listened to the ice grinding and groaning out on the bay as it fractured and ran aground—ice against rock and rock against ice. It must have sounded like this, ages and ages ago, when glaciers of ice carved away the ground, moving earth and stone, pushing up mountains and hollowing out canyons.

Despite the thrill of the wind, the arrival of spring, and the ice going out, I felt hope slowly seep out of me, leaving me cold and empty. I listened as the ice heaved toward shore, little glacier upon little glacier. It would have been one of the best sounds imaginable, the sound of winter *finally* ending, had Dad been safely asleep in the room across the hall. Instead, he was out there somewhere in all that grinding, shifting ice.

I padded barefoot to the window and leaned against

the sill, holding my breath so that I didn't fog the glass. In the gray, dusky light of the midnight sun, Hudson Bay had emerged, and the water now moved and heaved under the fractured ice, throwing it off like a winter coat.

Dad and his team had planned for this. They traveled by airboats specifically for the break up. And even though I knew this, I couldn't forget that Dad hadn't called. Each small island of ice making its way either shoreward or oceanward sank my own personal airboat of hope just a little more, taking my dad down with it.

I'd been having trouble falling asleep since Dad left, though I'd never said anything to Sura. Even if she asked, I would've blamed the old hot water radiator in my room. I didn't want to worry. I wanted to feel okay. I wanted my dad here and everything to be normal. I wanted him to sit out on the porch with me and listen to Simon sing and tell stories. I wanted him to be there when the Birdman took us out on bird-watching expeditions. I wanted him beside me at dinner, leaning back and stretching his long legs under the table. I wanted him now like I had wanted Mom. And didn't have either one of them.

I stood at the window, panic churning in the pit of my stomach.

Dad had been out there for a long time, suspended on ice between the arctic sky and the Arctic Sea. And there's a lot that can happen, even before the floes break up. Which is why Dad's call-ins had been so important. The last time he called, his voice scratchy and tied up in radio airwaves, he told me again that he'd be back before the ice went out.

But he wasn't back. And no one had heard from him.

Crawling into bed, I stared up at the ceiling. I tried not to let my imagination run wild. I refused to think about ice chasms and bitter storms that would make the already-chill temperatures drop even further. I refused to think about failing equipment, low supplies, or frostbite and hypothermia. But those things crept inside me anyway and pressed cold fingers against my heart till I could hardly breathe.

He isn't alone, I told myself. *His team is with him. They'll take care of each other. They'd let me know if something happened.*

But my fear hissed back, twisted and mean in the darkness.

Unless the equipment failed. Unless they're all dead.

Fear always says the worst things in the dark. And though I never meant to, I'd invited fear in, and now I couldn't make it leave.

Empty

FOUR DAYS LATER, THERE WERE no more loops left on my chain. I sat at the edge of Hudson Bay, facing north, knees pulled tight to my chest, my arms wrapped around them. I settled into the rocky shoreline. I would wait all day if necessary.

The warm wind pressed against my back as I searched out over the ice dams and across the open water for the tiny specks that I hoped would appear on the horizon—airboats bringing my dad home.

It was a strange sight, all that water dotted with ice. I'd never seen it before. Hudson Bay was *vast*. Not that the ice had made it smaller, just more crossable. Funny how just because I could walk on ice, it seemed less wild. Less dangerous. Like it was something I could handle. Something my dad could handle. But neither of us could walk on water.

The panic from last night had been replaced by the weight

of emptiness in the pit of my stomach. It was the same feeling I'd had when Mom died, and I hated that it was there. It's a terrible thing, really, being the one left behind.

Now it was Sunday, the day of our weekly call-ins. Dad made me promise only to call him in case of emergency, and Sura told me to give him the benefit of the doubt. I had listened to them both. But I couldn't anymore. The first week of July was over, and still Dad wasn't back. So if I didn't hear from him at the usual time tonight, I'd radio in myself.

After a while, Sura came and sat with me. She brought my lunch out to the shore when I refused to come back to the blue house. Some kind of meat stew in an oversized tin cup. I had no idea what kind of meat it was. Caribou? Rabbit? Seal? And suddenly I hated it. I hated everything about it. It was bits and pieces of this rock-strewn, frozen, ice-bound Arctic. And I was supposed to swallow it down and like it. The stew. This place. This place that had stolen my dad and might not give him back. I couldn't do it.

Before I could think of a reason not to, I threw the cup and all of its contents down the shore as far as I could. I didn't even care that Sura was right there beside me. I thought she would be mad, but she wasn't. She just sat with me and didn't say a word. She didn't even ask me to bring back the cup. So I didn't. I left it there on the shore until the tide eventually came in and carried it away.

Just before she left, Sura pulled something from her pocket

and handed it to me. A small feather, no larger than my thumb, and white as the moon over Hudson Bay. Pinching my fingers, I zipped the feather through them, straightening all of the tiny shafts until not a single one was out of place.

"It's the flight feather of an arctic tern," she told me. "He dropped it and I thought you might want it. To help you practice your flying."

I didn't understand.

"We forget," she said. "How to fly. It's a fragile thing, and the weight of things—things that hurt—can make us forget how it's done. We dream about it. We remember how it feels to be weightless. But once we forget, we have to spend the rest of our lives relearning how to take that leap and believe we can do it."

Sura had been staring out at the water, but she turned to me now. "If you can practice along the way," she said, "that first leap—the letting go—will be a little easier."

I was still confused—let go of what? Fear? Hope? Dad?—but I brushed the feather across my cheek, taking comfort in the softness against my skin.

Later, a few hours after Sura left, and after Simon, too, had come and gone, the Birdman showed up. Together we sat watching the tide creep up the shore, and every once in a while we would throw a few smooth stones as hard as we could out over the ice dams and into the open water. Sometimes they made it. Sometimes they didn't, landing among the embankments and steeples of ice with a hollow ricocheting sound.

Neither one of us said a word the whole time. We didn't need to.

Finally, the Birdman sighed, and handed me the binoculars that had been hanging around his neck. Then he got up, his bones creaking as they adjusted to standing, and left me on the bank alone.

I used the Birdman's binoculars to stare out over the water until there was no longer enough light to even imagine I was seeing something.

I stretched, stiff from sitting there all day, and lay down, folding my arms behind my head. There were no stars out yet. It wouldn't be dark enough to see them for a while, but I looked for them anyway. I knew they were there, behind the lingering arctic daylight.

I never wished on stars, they always seemed too far away. And most of them had already died long ago, so distant that all that remained was their light, still shooting through space and time to reach us. It made me wonder: What kind of light might I leave trailing out behind me, after I was gone?

When I couldn't stand the silence or the sight of all that empty water a minute longer, I stood up, tired and cold, and walked back to the blue house.

Sura was sitting in the front room waiting up for me, but

I stood in the entry, unlacing my boots and hanging up my coat very slowly. Taking years of time to do what should have taken just a few minutes.

I was afraid to look at her. She was sitting there so quietly, waiting for me, and it made the fear that had churned in my stomach all day long threaten to rise up and suffocate me. I brushed the feather she'd given me nervously across my cheek.

"It's almost eight," I said, and Sura nodded. Wordlessly we walked into the front room where Dad had set up the radio, and I stared at the map on the wall, trying not to look at the clock. Trying not to count the minutes, the seconds until the big hand reached the twelve. But it did. And then I stared at the radio, every part of me waiting.

Sura was absolutely silent beside me and we both held our breath. The only noise in the room was the clock's ticking second hand. I refused to look at the time again. I didn't want to know how many minutes past eight it was.

I stood there for what felt like forever, until Sura finally sighed, and I jumped and glanced at the clock: 8:42 P.M. I grabbed the radio receiver. Missing this many calls felt like an emergency.

My hands were shaking as I cleared my throat and held down the receiver button, filling the silence of the front room with the sound of my voice, tense and nervous.

"VE4 portable W1APL, come in. Over."

I let up on the receiver button and waited several long seconds before trying again. "VE4 portable W1APL, come in. Over."

Nothing.

"VE4 portable W1APL, this is Tal. Come in. Over." Radio static filled the front room in the blue house.

"Dad. This is Tal. Come in. Over." I could barely get the words around the lump in my throat.

Sura rested a hand on my shoulder and my stomach lurched, then sank too fast. I was on some kind of terrible roller coaster in the middle of the Arctic. My head ached. But I wouldn't cry. I *wouldn't*.

I looked at up at Sura. So steady. Same as those glacial rocks that dotted the tundra. But even those rocks had been moved, I guess. Set down and abandoned by the passage of massive icebergs, twisting and tearing their way through the landscape. Those rocks were moraine. And Sura was, too. She, too, had been left behind. Like me. Maybe we were all moraine—just pieces left over after everything else was gone. And with that thought I was suddenly very, very tired. I hung up the receiver, cutting off the sound of static, and then stood up carefully. I felt like if I moved too fast I might break into pieces. Sura reached for me, but then let her hands fall to her sides.

"I'm going to bed," I whispered, leaving a piece of myself on the stairs as I went.

Cut Short

I STOOD IN THE MIDDLE of my room for a few minutes, listening to the clunking of the radiator, the sound of my shaky breathing, and my crazy-beating heart, waiting for something steady. But even my own heartbeat was wrong, pounding too fast.

Why? *Why?* Why hadn't he answered? Why hadn't he come back? Why wasn't he already here? I twisted myself around the question, trying to make it work out right. I wanted an answer. To know what happened. I wanted to make my heart quit hurting, and maybe if I just knew *something*, it would help.

Out of habit, I glanced at the corner of my window alcove where my paper chain had hung. It looked empty there, now that the loops had run out. Not that it mattered. Not anymore. I never knew how many days he'd be gone anyway! So really, it was stupid. The whole thing. I'd just made it all up to make myself feel better. And look where that got me.

My young mom watched me from her frame on the top of my bookshelf. Her short hair hung at her chin like some kind of prophecy, taunting me with the notion that I was the one who would cut it all off. She smiled. Smiled and smiled, and never cared. Never cared that she left. Never cared that I didn't get to say good-bye.

I could feel my heart racing. Faster and faster. It wouldn't slow down. My ears rang with the sound of my own heartbeat. Loud. Too loud. It was drowning everything else out. *Lub-dub. Lub-dub. Lub-dub.* It was filling me up. Filling my room. *Lub-dub. Lub-dub.* I couldn't stop. Not this, not any of it. *Lub-dub.* Couldn't catch my. Breath. Had to. *Stop.*

I grabbed a pair of scissors from my desk.

Without even pausing, I took a handful of my hair and sheared it off.

The room went quiet, and my hair fell, long strands splaying across the wide-plank floorboards. And then I dropped the scissors, filling my room with the sound of their clatter.

I glanced at my mom's picture on the shelf.

Everyone is afraid of what they're unable to control.

I jumped when Sura knocked on the door.

"Talia, are you okay? I heard—" Her words cut short,

blunt at the ends as she took one look at me and then at the hair on the floor.

"It's okay!" My voice sounded funny and I leaned against my desk so she wouldn't see my hands shaking. "I wanted it short—off—it was too long, you know?—Too long. Too much. In my face and—and I needed it gone so—"

My words were getting all mixed up. Sura's arms caught me, held me tight before I could say anything else.

I stood there for a minute, stiff. Wanting her to believe I was fine. *I knew what I was doing. I'd meant it. I'd meant those scissors.* But being brave is harder than you ever think it's going to be, and despite what Sura thought, I couldn't fly. I was no tern. I was moraine. Only bits of me left behind. I couldn't do this. I couldn't lose them both.

I pressed my cheek against Sura's shoulder, feeling everything begin to crumble inside of me. My resolve, my determination, my hope. Wrapping my arms around her, I quit fighting the lump in my throat. It was just too hard.

Finally, after all this time, I let myself cry.

I cried for Mom because she was never coming back. I cried for Dad because he had lost so much, and I cried for me because I couldn't do this alone.

The weight of all my waiting and wishing washed over me like a giant wave off Hudson Bay, determined to pull me under. It was too much, and no matter how many times I told myself that nothing could ever be as bad as losing Mom, I didn't believe it anymore. Losing my dad would be just as awful.

After we stood there like that awhile, and after I calmed down some, Sura pulled away and held me at arm's length, her head tilted to one side as she considered my hair.

"I think you've started a good thing here, Talia. What do you say we finish it?"

I fingered the ends of my hair. I'd cut more than I meant to. A lot more. But I nodded, and Sura pulled my desk chair into the bathroom.

Sitting there in the tiny bathroom on the second floor of the blue house, I watched Sura's reflection in the bathroom mirror. I watched her face as she pulled my hair off my neck and over the back of the chair, hanging long to the middle of my back. She combed her fingers through it, the ends stringy and broken from where I had chewed. It hadn't been trimmed since Mom died. Last March. She'd been the last person to cut it.

I closed my eyes as Sura laid the scissors against my hair. The same scissors I used to make my paper chain calendar. The same scissors I'd used to cut tiny paper slips for my jar of wishes.

Snip. Snip. Snip-snip. Snip.

Sura began where I'd started with that first desperate chop, working around my head until it was even, falling just past my ears. And when she was finished, she rested her hands on my shoulders.

"Okay," Sura said gently. "You can open your eyes."

I met my gaze in the mirror.

"You still look like her," she said after a minute, her voice low and smooth as chocolate. "But you look more like you now. More yourself."

I studied my face, trying to see what Sura did. But I couldn't shake off thoughts of Dad.

"What am I going to do if he doesn't come back? If he's really gone—?" My voice quit working and I stared down at the strands of hair on the floor.

"Let's give him the benefit of the doubt, Talia," Sura said. She was firm. "It's possible that something unexpected is keeping him, so let's trust, for now at least, that he is on his way. Let's trust he knows how to do this thing on both ice and waves. And until we have concrete proof of something else, we are going to wait for him to come back. Okay?"

I held her gaze in the mirror, wanting what she had. Wanting her faith.

But I didn't have that, so I just said, "Okay."

Sura left me in my room sometime later, a cup of chaithluk tea by my bed. I couldn't sleep, so I stood at the window for a long time, staring out into the lingering arctic summer light, wishing and waiting.

Narwhals

THAT NIGHT I DREAMED ABOUT the auroras—the northern lights.

I'd first seen them on my birthday. But the night after the ice went out on Hudson Bay, the night that Sura cut my hair, I dreamed about a very different type of aurora and about Sura's story. Instead of spirit guides with upheld torches, thousands of beluga whales swam through dark skies. They sent ripples across the starscape as they broke the surface to breathe. The whoosh of their held breath escaping into the blackness was comforting, a living sound, warm and heavy. Light from the stars reflected against their white bodies, and in my dream, they led my mom across the abyss into that place where pain and disease no longer exist.

I woke sometime close to dawn with the dream of white whales fresh in my mind. I could still see Mom, her long hair splayed out around her as she swam through a black sky, buoyed up and carried across by whales.

I heard the muffled murmur of quiet voices from downstairs, which was strange and alarming considering how early it was.

I sat up in bed, listening. A chill that had nothing to do with the cold slid down my body. I took deep breaths. A dark and familiar dread tugged at me. Someone was here. Word had come—news of Dad. There was no other reason Sura would be up so early. Or maybe she'd never gone to bed at all.

Whenever the news is bad, adults talk in low, solemn voices, even when they're in the same room with you. It's like they think that by changing their tone, they can soften the weight of their words.

I listened for that lowness. Solemn notes that would tell me what I was so afraid of. But Sura's voice was warm. She *laughed*. And then a deeper voice chimed in.

Dad.

I was out of bed and halfway down the stairs before I even realized I'd moved.

He sat in a chair beside the wood stove, his feet stretched toward the warmth. His wool sweater and gray wool trousers were both familiar and strange at the same time. His face was red from sun- and windburn, and his lips were cracked from the cold. His beard was thicker and longer than it had been when he left, but his eyes were the same bright blue, and they lit up when he saw me on the stairs.

Before he could say my name, I was in his arms, and I wrapped myself around him and held on, tight. It was hard to breathe, like I'd been running for a long time. My heart pounded against my ribs and my ears roared as I struggled to catch my breath.

He held me close and we stood there in the middle of the room for a long time. He kept saying *shhh* over and over again, even though I wasn't crying. I felt like a snow globe. Someone had shaken me up and sent everything inside of me swirling around, and now, here in my dad's arms, was the stillness.

Finally, Dad settled back into his chair by the fire. But even then I couldn't let go of him. My fingers turned white as I gripped his shirt.

"The ice broke up faster than we'd anticipated," Dad said quietly. "I didn't want to risk getting caught and crushed in the floes, so we waited it out on one of the tiny islands offshore of Baffin. Once the ice broke up, I had no way of getting word to you. I'm so sorry, Tal. I'm so sorry I worried you."

Dad always carried the radio phone with him, charging it with the gas-powered generator when the team set up camp. But when they tore everything down and moved locations, it lost battery power very quickly on account of the cold. And they couldn't use the generator in the boat, so when they headed for home, the radio was useless long before they made it back to Churchill.

"It took much longer than I expected," Dad said. "I'm so sorry, Talia. I never meant to put you through that." He squeezed me tight against his chest.

I bit my lip and nodded. His words ricocheted around inside my head, bouncing off and echoing one another, like an Inuit throat song inside me. He'd waited. To be safe. And he was. But I still didn't let go of him.

I slowly relaxed my grip and just rested there in his lap, watching the fire flicker in the grate, feeling the rise and fall of his chest against my cheek. He smelled of ocean and sweat and that particular smell that was all his own, and I took it in.

I could breathe again. Until then I hadn't even realized I'd been holding my breath. Now, with Dad back safe and sound, my heart didn't feel like it was jumping around quite so much.

We sat in silence for a while, Dad and me by the fire, while Sura sat across the room on the couch, her eyes large and dark as she watched us.

"For nearly two weeks we searched for belugas, Tal." His voice was filled with a mixture of frustration and confusion and he ran a hand through his hair, long and in need of a cut. "We found nothing," he said. "*Nothing.* There were no whales where there should have been whales all along."

I frowned and thought of my dream, wondering if it was

worth mentioning, but Dad's voice took on a new note and he rested his chin against the top of my head.

"And then, on June thirteenth, on your birthday, Tal, we picked up whale song."

Across the room, the light of the fire caught the gleam of Sura's eyes. She looked as enthralled by Dad's story as I did.

"We watched the edge of the floes all morning, knowing they would surface there, sooner or later. And they did," Dad continued. "Right around sunrise, Tal, a single white horn, six feet long, rose up out of the water, and then another."

I gasped and pushed off his chest so I could see his face.

"Narwhals! No belugas from here to Greenland, but we found unicorns!" Dad laughed, exultant.

For two and a half weeks, Dad and his team followed a pod of fourteen whales—nine cows, two bulls, and three juveniles. But when the ice started breaking up, the team was forced back to shore.

"I'm hoping to go back out and see if we can't find them again," Dad said. "Soon. I was thinking maybe you'd like to come along?"

I stared into his face, trying to decide if he was serious.

Just then the wishes in my jar, still hidden beneath my bed upstairs, started rustling so loudly I was surprised no one else heard them.

Before I could even respond that yes, *yes,* I wanted to

come, Dad said suddenly, "You cut your hair." More a question than a statement.

I just nodded. "Sura helped me get it straight. Do you like it?"

"I like it," Dad said. He didn't say I looked like Mom, but that was okay.

By the time I'd calmed down and heard enough of Dad's expedition to make me drowsy, morning had officially arrived, though the sun had been up since three o'clock.

Sura made hot chocolate with extra marshmallows, and my mug—the blue one with the spiraling white handle—was nearly empty. Only a bit of thick dark chocolate remained swirling at the bottom.

None of us felt like starting our day after being awake for so many hours, so we decided to pretend the sun wasn't actually up. Sura drew the shades in the front room and Dad scooped me up and carried me upstairs to bed.

Who would have guessed that after such a terrible, horrible, lonely day, the next would begin with so much hope? Dad had come back to me. There were unicorns almost close enough to touch. And my wish—my biggest wish ever—was about to come true.

I rested my head against his shoulder, enjoying the feel of his whiskery face against mine. And as he tucked me into bed and closed my curtains against the morning sun, I told him about the dream I'd had about Mom.

He said nothing, just listening while a kind of half-sad smile played around his eyes.

When I finished, he said, "Tal, I can think of no better place for our missing white whales."

Then he tucked the covers around me, but paused for a second when he noticed I was wearing the necklace.

"Do you like your birthday present?"

"I love it!" I said. "How did you know?"

"How did I know what?"

"About me and unicorns?"

He shrugged. "I know you love that story Mom used to read to you. And I know it's important to believe good things can happen, even when life doesn't feel good."

I nodded slowly. "But how do you do that? I mean, really?" I fingered the ends of my hair. "I didn't think you were coming back, Dad—" I swallowed hard, wanting to hang on to him again. "And no matter how hard I stared out at the water or how many times I told myself you'd be back, I was still afraid."

"I'm sorry." His voice was sort of choky. "I was afraid, too."

"You were afraid?"

"Of course. What, I'm not allowed to be scared sometimes?"

"I guess you can be scared." I smiled, smoothing out the edge of my quilt.

For some reason it seemed strange that my dad would be

scared of anything—like, *actually* scared. He'd been going to faraway places and making his own adventures for as long as I could remember.

"What were you scared of?" I asked.

"I was afraid of losing you," he said. "I still am."

"But I'm right here! I never went anywhere!" I stared at him, trying to read behind his eyes. I'd always been right here. He was the one who'd left.

He nodded like he was trying to reassure me, and then stared out my bedroom window for a minute.

"Tal, just because you're afraid of something doesn't mean you aren't brave," he said. "It just means you've learned to recognize the things that can hurt you. Bravery is choosing to believe in the possibility of good things—beautiful things—even when you feel afraid." He paused. "Your mom taught me that."

Then he leaned down and kissed my forehead, and pulled a small handheld tape recorder from his pocket—the kind journalists use when doing interviews.

"I have something for you," he said, holding it up. "Listen." And he pushed Play.

There was nothing at first, and then a quiet whooshing—the sound of water from beneath the surface, and then without warning, a kind of high-pitched wail, like a woman humming off-key.

Whale song.

Dad had taped the narwhals' song for me, and I sat up in bed, listening as it poured from the recorder into my room. Harmonies belonging only to the sea filled the upstairs room in the blue house, and my heart was swept away. Unfamiliar sounds rose and fell, some deep and resounding, while others climbed, rich and high and sweet.

We listened to them, Dad and I, as the sun shone bright over Hudson Bay. And I made him play the recording twice more before I finally fell asleep to the sounds of unicorns singing.

Pancakes and Things Worth Wanting

WHEN I WOKE UP it was already late afternoon, but Dad and Sura were still sleeping. I slipped quietly out of bed and tiptoed down the hall to Dad's room. I needed to be sure he was actually there. I needed to be sure I hadn't dreamed him.

Turning the doorknob so it wouldn't squeak, I cracked the door and peeked in. And sure enough, there he was, sound asleep, one arm thrown over his face against the afternoon light. I couldn't help but smile. I closed the door still grinning, and padded downstairs in my wool socks, careful not to wake anyone.

I'd never made pancakes on my own before, but I'd watched

Mom and now Sura make them often enough to give it a try. I dug through the pantry until I found the flour, sugar, salt, and baking powder, and piled the ingredients on the counter along with milk and eggs from the fridge. Mixing everything together until I had a smooth batter, I placed a skillet on the stove and carefully poured the batter into a nice little circle.

It took several tries before I got it right. The pan was too hot at first and I burned the first couple pancakes. But I had a nice stack growing on a plate beside the stove when Sura cleared her throat from somewhere behind me. I found her leaning against the doorframe, her arms folded across her chest and a smile pulling at her eyes.

"If I knew you were this handy in the kitchen, I would have put you to work much sooner," she said.

I laughed, a little nervous. "Hope it's okay—I just wanted to do something special."

"It's fine!" she said. "And it looks like you're doing a pretty good job." She eyed the stack of pancakes. "There's just one thing missing."

I glanced at the ingredients still strewn across the counter. What had I forgotten? But Sura shook her head. "Coffee," she said. "We need coffee."

"Think I'll stick to hot chocolate."

Sura smiled and filled the teakettle at the sink.

We didn't have to wait long before we heard Dad moving around upstairs, the floorboards creaking under him.

"I smell pancakes!" he said as he came down the stairs.

"Tal made them," Sura said, handing him a cup of coffee.

"By myself," I added. Because I wanted him to know I was different, I'd grown up—just a little—while he was gone.

I watched Dad as he ate, his legs stretched out under the table. He was just as I remembered him, and he smiled across the table at me, mopping up the last bit of syrup with one final bite.

"Those were good, Tal. Really good." He sighed and pushed back his plate. "So what do you say—are you up for finding some unicorns?"

"Now?" I gasped, and Dad grinned. I could hardly believe this was happening.

"Yes now," he said. "You've got thirty minutes to get your things together. There's still ice out there on the water." He paused, his voice taking on a serious note. "But a pod of narwhals is waiting for you about a two days' boat ride from here, and I'm not going to let a little ice stand between you and those whales."

I smiled. There were unicorns waiting for *me*.

While we slept, Dad's crew had spent the morning restocking supplies and getting things ready to go back out on the water. He had gotten special permission for me to come along.

We met them at the landing in town where a ferry named *The Walrus* waited to take us out. It was named after that sad, silly poem by Lewis Carroll, and as he loaded our stuff, Dad recited a few lines.

"'The time has come,' the Walrus said, 'to talk of many things: Of shoes—and ships—and sealing wax—of cabbages—and kings . . .'" It was a funny thing for him to do, because it was exactly the sort of thing Mom would have done.

"So, what do you think? You ready?" Dad dropped my duffel next to his and leaned against the boat rail beside me.

Was I ready? I'd been waiting for this moment for weeks, so the fact that I had to stop and think about it for a minute seemed strange. But from the moment I'd stepped onto the dock I'd been trying to sort out what I was feeling, exactly.

I closed my eyes, inhaling deeply, trying to take it all in. I smelled briny salt and underwater vegetation mixed with fish and crustaceans. Flounder, crab, shrimp, newly melted ice and sunshine, and gasoline fumes from the ferry. Beneath all those obvious things, deep down there somewhere, was my pod of narwhal whales—unicorns—old and magic. I exhaled and opened my eyes, running my hands nervously along the cold rail that separated me from the icy waters of Hudson Bay.

"I'm ready," I said, smiling up at Dad. "Definitely ready."

This was good, being here with him. Feeling the rush of wind and salt that blew my new short hair away from my face. It was all good. But as I turned and glanced over my shoulder, I also felt like I was leaving a part of myself on shore.

Since my birthday, something had changed. Somehow, over the past several weeks, I'd discovered parts of myself I didn't know were there. And now while one half of me was about to venture out onto Hudson Bay with my dad, the other half wanted to stay in Churchill with my friends. At the kitchen table with Sura. Wandering down some back road with the Birdman, his binoculars around my neck. And especially with Simon—Simon and all of his songs.

I couldn't imagine what Churchill would have been like if they hadn't been here, and as excited as I was to finally be with Dad, to be one step closer to finding my unicorn, I felt a little sad.

I wrapped my arms around myself, fighting off the chill that raced across the open water, and turned to face the sea.

I tried to shake off this strange mix of feelings, but I couldn't get Simon out of my head. I kept seeing his face, his grin, and the way his hair stuck up off just one side of his head. Our wishes had come true—my birthday wish and Simon's skipping-rock wish. There were unicorns off Baffin Island, and I couldn't leave without telling him.

"I need to do something before we go," I told Dad. "I'll be really quick!" And before he had a chance to argue, I bolted from the ferry. "Don't leave without me!" I called, but he just stood there at the rail, a confused expression furrowing his brow.

The house the Birdman and Simon were renting for the summer wasn't that far from the landing, and I raced there as fast as I could. I had to tell Simon about the whales. About Dad. About everything. I needed him to know that my wish— *our* wishes—had come true.

I ran up the porch steps, pounding on the door, and nearly fell over the threshold when Simon jerked it open.

"My dad came in last night! He's alive and he's fine, and there are narwhal whales off Baffin Island," I said breathlessly. "Unicorn whales! And I'm leaving now with my dad to see them. But I couldn't leave without telling you. Without saying good-bye!"

"Well I hope not!" he exclaimed, and he grabbed me in a hug that was one part relief and all parts happy. "Pretty sure we couldn't be friends anymore if you just up and left without telling me something as great as all that."

I stepped back, my face flushed from the wind and my run and the warmth of his hug.

"See?" he said. "I told you your dad was fine!"

"Yes, you did."

"I'm almost always right. You should listen to me more often."

I laughed.

"I have to go." I thumbed toward the landing. "Dad's waiting and I said I'd be quick."

Simon nodded. "Come back, okay?"

"Promise," I said. "You want me to make any wishes for you, while I'm out there?" Doing so would break rule number two. But I didn't really care that only my wishes were supposed to go into my jar.

"Nah. I'm good." He shook his head. "I've already got everything I want."

"Really?" I asked.

He shrugged. "I've got everything that counts," he said. "And I guess that's pretty good."

Mom's words swirled around me for a minute, tossed by the wind sweeping in off the bay.

The happiest people are the ones who've decided that everything they already have is everything they'll ever want.

And she was right.

Hope is a Bird

THE WALRUS HEADED TOWARD Baffin Island, where a small whaling boat waited to take us into the island inlets. Dad's team had sighted narwhals there only a week ago.

One week. How far could a unicorn swim in a week?

Three miles? Thirty?

"They won't go far," Dad said, "if their food source is good."

So I closed my eyes, crossed my fingers, and wished for shrimp. Hundreds of shrimp. *Millions.* And cod. And whatever else they ate. That way, those whales wouldn't have to move a single inch. They could just stay right where they were and wait for me.

Beneath sweaters and wool socks, my jar waited at the bottom of my duffel bag. Every once in a while I was sure I heard my wishes rustling around over the rush of the arctic wind. They'd come alive again since my dad's return, and they had taken on new life out here. So when I saw that long white horn rise up out of the arctic water for myself, I'd open that jar and empty my wishes into the sea.

It would take us a day to reach Baffin Island aboard the ferry, and another day to reach the spot where the whales had last been seen. If we were lucky enough to see them ourselves, Dad wanted to follow them and learn as much as he could about the pod. But only if the weather held. It was still dangerous out here. Even though the ice had already broken up, leaving only a stray iceberg here and there, the weather could turn in a matter of minutes, throwing the relatively calm sea into raging turmoil. I could only hope that wouldn't affect our chances of finding the pod.

Lucky for me, whales stick by each other, look out for one another, and pretty much behave like a family. They're very social creatures, so whenever you hear about a whale off all alone, you can be pretty sure it got separated from its pod. That meant chances were good that I would see more than one narwhal.

There were young whales with this particular group, which, Dad told me, meant it was a healthy family. They had enough to eat and enough freedom from predators to feel safe.

"Young whales are always a good thing," Dad said.

"The more narwhals swimming around the Arctic Sea, the greater chance I'll have to study them."

And the greater chance my wishes would be granted.

"But if we don't see the whales," Dad said, "if we search and can't find them within five days, then we'll turn around and go back to Churchill. It took us two days to get here and it will take two to get back, granted the weather holds. I don't want you out here any longer than necessary, and nine days on a whaling boat on the Arctic Sea is more than enough."

Dad cared about my safety more than he cared about my happiness. And even though five days wasn't very long, it was enough time to find my narwhals. It had to be.

The morning we were set to arrive at Baffin Island, Dad and I braved the cold and stood on deck, looking out into the bay. Dad was smiling, his eyes watering from the bite of the wind. I knew he was worried about keeping me safe, but still, he *wanted* me here with him. He really did. And I didn't realize how great it would be just knowing that.

I gripped the rail, the cold seeping through my mittens. I knew the Arctic Sea was a dangerous place, even for an experienced team of researchers. That was obvious every time I looked over the ferry's rail into the dark water.

Being out here wasn't dangerous just because of the cold water and icy temperatures, though. It was also dangerous be-

cause Hudson Bay and all of her surrounding inlets and channels, basins, and uncharted depths were unpredictable. Dad
couldn't guarantee anything. He told me that. No matter how
hard we looked, there was a possibility that we wouldn't see
those unicorn whales. And without them, there would be no
granted wishes.

I held myself steady against the cold wind and sea spray,
and the possibility of disappointment. I'd been holding out
for this a long time. Hoping. Since that first week in Churchill, actually. Maybe even before. I just hadn't known what
I was looking for back then.

But here's the thing about hope. You're not guaranteed much.
Not ever. That's what makes it such a beautiful and terrible
thing. Despite your determination, or how hard you believe, or
the number of wishes in your jar, hope, like a tern, can fly straight
into your outstretched hands, or it can fly just out of reach.

As we sailed on, Dad and I rode through the wide channels
and inlets that bridged Baffin Island and Greenland. The
cold water and gray skies were interrupted only by occa-
sional whitecaps, stray massive chunks of ice, and an endless
parade of seabirds, curious and hungry.

I was hungry, too, but for something else entirely. I pictured
the shape of those waters on the map that hung on my bedroom wall. Fingers of water pressed into Baffin Island on the
south and into Greenland on the north, like misshapen hands

pushing up against the land masses, holding back what I was hoping to see.

On the evening of the second day, we traded our ferry for a small whaling boat on the shores of Baffin Island to help us navigate the seas better. I curled up my body as tight as I could against the cold, fists buried in my underarms as I tried to coax heat from my body. But even wrapped in wool sweaters and a goose-down parka, I couldn't keep my teeth from jumping against each other. I was freezing. Dad was, too. Every time he stepped out on deck, icicles formed on his beard and frost collected in his hair and eyebrows—the frozen fog of his own breath.

Inside the cabin, a map was pinned to the wall, speckled with dots and connecting lines. It was twin to my own map, except this one had the addition of several small stars. These marked the locations Dad had sighted narwhals.

On the morning of the third day we reached the place where Dad had marked his first star. We had five days to find whales. I kissed my fingertip and pressed it against the mark.

This is it, I thought. *This is where the magic happens.*

We immediately started dropping booms into the water, holding our breath and pressing our hands over the headphones covering our ears—like it would improve the quality of sound pouring in from ocean currents beneath the boat.

Adjusting the dial sensitivity on the receivers and repeatedly checking our location, Dad and I were relentless. We didn't even take a break for lunch; we just kept going, moving in wider and wider circles around that first star on the map, like some kind of small water-bound moon circling our own invisible sun.

But the sea was quiet.

Just before dark we reached the location of the second star Dad had marked on his map. I started getting the booms ready again, but he stopped me.

"Talia, it's late," he said. "You haven't eaten anything since breakfast and we need to take a break for the night. If the whales are here now, they'll be here in the morning."

"If the whales are here? *If?*" I asked, my chest tightening. My voice sounded loud. Too loud. "They have to be here!" I insisted, clearing my throat and lowering my voice. "We can't stop now, not when we're so close."

"No one is giving up, Tal," Dad said. "I'm glad you're so enthusiastic about the whales, but we won't last four more days if we try to keep this pace through the night, and don't forget, we have to make it back to Churchill, too. Come on. Help me make dinner. We'll try again in the morning."

I was so reluctant to stop the search that Dad eventually had to insist, gently taking the boom cables from my hands and winding them back up in their crates. Although I didn't want to, I finally gave in, and helped him put away the equipment. If I put up too much of a fight, his surprise at my commitment might turn to concern or frustration, or worse, curiosity.

Even though Dad knew about me and unicorns, I wasn't ready to explain my jar of wishes just yet. I was worried he wouldn't understand. Sometimes a secret gets better when you share it, and sometimes telling a secret makes it smaller. I couldn't afford to have my belief in unicorns shrink just when I was about to see them. We still had four whole days left to search, and just because we hadn't found the whales today didn't mean we wouldn't find them tomorrow.

But the next day was no better.

And neither was the day after that.

All day we orbited the second star on the map in ever-widening circles. And then we did the same surrounding the third star Dad had marked. With chattering teeth and shaking fingers I turned the knobs and dials on the receiver myself, while Dad lowered booms into the Arctic Sea. And with every ounce of strength I possessed, I poured my whole self into listening, waiting to hear whale song. Waiting for the voices of my unicorns. But they did not sing for me.

In the midst of all that cold, where gray skies pressed down on gray, empty water, I tasted the same disappointment Dad must have felt, searching for his belugas and never finding them. Even my wishes, written across dozens of tiny paper slips, had gone still in their jar. Silent.

And the sea remained quiet. Empty. By the middle of the fourth day it was all I could do to keep from screaming, *"Where are you? You're supposed to be here!"*

But I didn't scream, or cry. Instead I just stared up at the cloud-filled skies as they bore down against my chest, and I whispered one word, over and over and over again until Dad rested his heavily mittened hand on my shoulder. I jerked away from him, throwing myself against the prow of our little whaling boat, whispering that one word in my heart.

Please. Please. Please.

It became a kind of prayer. A prayer that went un-answered.

Unfair

AS DAYLIGHT FADED AWAY on the evening of the fifth day, Dad stood on deck beside me in the cold wind, and together we searched the dark, empty seascape. Beginning at sunrise we would start making our way back to Baffin Island and then Churchill.

Even though Dad was standing right next to me, I felt alone. This was different for him. He was used to this. The hope, the search, the disappointment. And then he would try again. But this was my only chance.

Dad didn't need the unicorns the same way I did. He didn't have a jar filled up with wishes, one of which needed granting more than anything else. He didn't still need her. Not like I did.

But none of that mattered now because they weren't here. There were no unicorns.

I began carefully hauling in the booms, my back to the empty sea, ocean water splashing on the deck and onto my boots as I heaved the long cables up over the rail. Even with the protective waterproof choppers, it only took a few minutes before my hands were frozen and I couldn't feel my fingertips anymore. Dad came and took a cable from me, hauling it hand over hand and winding it into a neat coil on the deck until the heavy boom attached to the cable's end reached the surface. And he hauled it over the rail as well, his strong arms making it all look so easy.

"You okay, Tal?" he asked.

"I'm fine," I said. But I was clenching my teeth and holding back tears, so the words came out funny.

I didn't at look at him. I wanted him to go away so I could just be angry instead of sad. Because somehow that was easier. Sad brought everything closing in around me until I couldn't breathe anymore, or think straight—even if I wanted to. So I chose angry instead. I was angry at Dad for being gone, at the whales for not being there at all, at myself for hoping, at Mom for dying. And I was almost sure Dad would turn around and walk away. Because, maybe, that was easier for him.

But he didn't.

With his arms full of equipment he stood there behind me, his tall frame swaying easily with the motion of the rocking boat.

"I know this is hard," he said.

When I didn't respond right away, he sighed. Then he said, "I miss her, too, Talia."

The wind caught his words and threw them out to sea, and my stomach dropped as they floated away. I wanted to hang on to them, to write them on a slip of paper so I could keep them. I hadn't realized how desperately I needed to hear him say that—to hear Dad say he missed her. And it wasn't fair of me to be mad at him for never having said it before because I never talked about Mom, either. It was the one wish I'd never made, and maybe I should have. Maybe I should have been wishing it all along.

I wish we could talk about Mom.

"Talia. Look at me." Dad's voice was quiet and firm.

But I couldn't look at him. Instead, I took a deep breath and let it out slowly, making myself swallow the tears.

"You think you're the only one who's hurting?" Dad asked, setting down his equipment and coming to stand beside me. I was surprised by the bite of frustration that iced over his words. "You think you're the only one who would give just about anything to have Mom back?" His voice shook and his mittened hands gripped the guardrail. "I know I haven't been there for you as much as I should have been," he said, "and I might be getting more things wrong than right, but I sure as hell know you're not *fine*."

I bit my lip and stared, dry-eyed, over the water.

"I'm doing the best I can, Tal," he said. "I know this is hard, for both of us, but I'm figuring this out as I go. And I'm right here now. You don't have to do this alone."

It wasn't until then that I actually looked at him.

"You're *right here*?" The threat of tears vanished, swallowed up by the hotness rising in my chest. "I've been on my own for weeks! You went off to look for whales, and you just left me!"

"I know," he said. "I know, and I'm sorry."

"You're sorry? No! That's not fair! That doesn't just fix everything!"

"I can't fix this!" Dad said. "And you're right! It isn't fair. Nothing about this is fair. Losing Mom wasn't fair. Coming here, that wasn't fair to you. The missing belugas aren't fair. Leaving you with Sura wasn't fair—for either of you. And now we can't find those narwhals, and that's not fair, either. Life isn't fair, Talia! And no matter what I do, no matter how sorry I am, I can't fix this for you."

His voice had gone from angry to so quiet and low, I almost couldn't hear him over the noise of the water and the boat.

"If I knew how to fix it, I would. If I knew what you needed, I'd make sure you had it, Tal." He ran his hands over his head in frustration. "But I don't know what you need. I don't even know what *I* need."

I stared at the toes of my boots. The spray off the boat had glazed them in salt water.

"But I'm not giving up," Dad said. "I'm not leaving again. I'm not going anywhere without you. Okay? I promise." He turned, staring at the side of my face. "I want to try and figure this out. With you. I thought maybe bringing you out here would help get us started."

I pressed myself against the rail, closing my eyes and letting the wind whip salt spray over my skin. It was bitter cold and tasted like tears. And suddenly I wanted to tell him I didn't know what I needed either. I wanted to tell him how much I'd missed him. How much I missed Mom. How much I wanted everything to go back to the way it was before. I wanted to tell him to keep trying to figure things out. I wanted to tell him I was sorry, too, because no matter how much I didn't want to admit it, I knew that even if he'd stayed, even if we'd never come to Churchill, I still would have been angry and sad.

But I didn't say anything. I just stood there, staring out at the waves of salt water. And then, slowly, I leaned over and rested my head against his shoulder, fingering the tiny horn that hung around my neck on its delicate silver chain.

On the morning of the sixth day, we woke up early to do one final search. Then around lunchtime, when we still hadn't found anything, Dad officially called off our expedition, and we began making our way back to Baffin Island. We would stay there until the following morning when *The Walrus* would arrive and take us the rest of the way to Churchill.

Hours later when the boat finally docked, Dad had to nearly carry me to shore because I was so cold and stiff, and tired with disappointment. He wrapped his arms around me and kissed the top of my hair.

"I'm sorry," he said again.

I just shook my head and buried my face in his chest. For a minute I considered telling him about my jar so that he would know why those unicorn whales were so important. But I didn't.

We stayed the night on the island, huddled up next to small propane stoves and hot cups of coffee, which normally would have tasted too dark and bitter to me. That night the bitterness was exactly right. And although it wasn't fair, maybe it didn't have to be to still be okay. Maybe I wasn't supposed to find those unicorns just yet, because if I had, Dad never would have said the things he did. And maybe—maybe—I needed to hear those things, at least on this trip, more than I needed unicorns.

The Birdman
and the
Bear

AS DAD AND I DOCKED in Churchill and started hauling our equipment and supplies back to the CNSC, I felt
ready to get back to the blue house—to Sura, and Simon,
and the Birdman. We'd only been gone nine days, but I'd
missed them. More than I thought I would.

Dad and I didn't say much on the drive back to town,
but it wasn't as uncomfortable as before we left. Knowing he
still missed Mom, knowing he hadn't forgotten all about her,
knowing he wanted things to change between us had made the
Mom-sized space between us shift a little. Maybe even shrink.

Sura met us at the door and welcomed us back, and I actually gave her a hug, which surprised her I think. She started rushing around after that, helping us settle in, putting the kettle on the stove for coffee and hot chocolate, doing her best to make us feel like we'd come home. Which, in a way, we had.

"I'm going to put my stuff away," I called as I headed toward the stairs, but there were only muffled voices of response from the kitchen.

I made my way up the narrow stairway, hefting my duffel bag over my shoulder, my steps a bit clumsy in the steadiness of the house after the constant motion of the boat.

I dropped my bag on the bed and surveyed my room, welcoming and untouched in my absence. My books were stacked neatly on my shelf, my shoes lined against the wall by my closet. My corkboard hung over my desk—littered with bits of Churchill that represented something to me. I'd pinned up the arctic tern feather Sura had given me, her recipe for touton, and the words to "Baby Blue" that Simon had copied down.

I ran my finger along the edge of the tern's feather before sighing and unzipping my bag. A bundle of dirty clothes, socks, mittens, hats, and wool sweaters spilled out. And buried beneath it all, my jar of wishes sat silent and motionless.

All summer, I'd been waiting for that moment out on the water. But that moment had come and gone and my jar was still full. Now I didn't know what to do with it because this wasn't part of the plan. I didn't want to put it back under my bed. I was afraid its fullness would rise into me while I slept, filling me up with the weight of my unfulfilled wishes. But I couldn't just leave it sitting on top of my desk for everyone to see, either.

So I emptied my duffel of dirty clothes and left my jar where it was, in the bottom of the bag, zipping it up and stuffing the whole thing in the back of my closet.

After I brought my laundry downstairs and started a load in the wash, I wandered back toward the kitchen and leaned against the doorway, listening to Dad tell Sura about our expedition as she made dinner. And then I walked in, washed my hands in the sink, and began pulling apart a head of lettuce for the salad Sura was making.

I felt Dad's eyes on me and heard him falter briefly in whatever he was saying, but Sura wasn't fazed. She didn't make a fuss or tell me she didn't need my help, which was probably true. Instead, she just flashed me a warm smile and returned to the onions she was chopping.

We moved quietly around the kitchen, me slowly navigating the unfamiliar room, and Sura offering directions whenever I began to look a little lost. Like drawing lines between coordinate points on an uncharted map, I was slowly finding my way.

I glanced at Sura, watching her move around the kitchen. She made it look so easy, same as Simon playing his guitar, and I added a wish to my jar, writing it across a slip of paper in my mind.

I wish I could cook like Sura.

But as I watched her, I noticed that she looked different than usual. There was something not quite right—anxiousness hung around her eyes. Her eyebrows kept coming together as she worked, settling her face into a worried frown. Sura's kitchen was the one place where she was usually comfortable and totally at ease, and I suddenly wondered if it was me. Maybe I was in the way? But when she caught me looking at her, she smiled. I probably wouldn't have noticed the effort it took, except that I was used to people rearranging their faces around me. The doctors and nurses did it all the time while Mom was in the hospital, like by changing their expressions they could protect me from something. And a kind of heavy unease settled in my chest as I tried to shake the feeling that Sura was doing the same.

She waited until we finished dinner—salad with a light dressing, steaming bowls of caribou stew, and warm crusty bread fresh from the oven—before she told us what had happened.

"The Birdman was attacked by a bear." She said the words quiet and slow, like she was trying to ease them into the room and do as little damage as possible.

But the way she said "attacked" made the walls in the kitchen close in on me. There was a roaring in my ears, and Dad sat up very straight in his chair. All I could see was the face of that polar bear—nanuq—long and white, its black eyes small and steady as it gazed at me from the other side of the windshield.

Churchill's polar bears seemed especially attracted to the Birdman. None of us knew why. The Birdman obeyed all the rules, stuck to the roads, carried pepper spray, wore bells to signal his presence, and never provoked a bear. Perhaps he smelled particularly tasty.

"He's all right," Sura said, looking at me anxiously. "Or, he will be."

The Birdman had been just outside of town. It was early in the morning when a small road crew, working to repair some of the ice-damaged roads, heard someone screaming. They'd taken a truck over the tundra and not more than three hundred yards into the scrub, they found the Birdman getting worked on by a young bear.

Sura paused and glanced at Dad, and whatever passed between them made her skip the details. She told us how the bear had been shot right there in the scrub, and how the road crew had rushed the Birdman back to town. He was at the hospital now. Simon was with him.

That was all I needed to hear. I was out the door and racing for the Churchill Regional Health Authority building. I heard the screen door open and Dad call my name, but I gritted my teeth and didn't stop.

This was too big. Too urgent. Dad hadn't been here for the last six weeks. He didn't know Simon and the Birdman like I did. They were important. I had to go.

Uncontrollable Things

I RAN ALL THE WAY, and Dad caught up to me by car. I could tell he was upset with me for taking off, but he didn't say anything. He just drew his lips together in a straight line and sighed, running a hand through his hair. Together we walked into the hospital.

A nurse led us to the Birdman's room, but I hesitated. My legs had quit working. I was still out of breath from running, and now I was shaking, too, nervous and scared. I fell into a chair just outside his room. I needed to make my stomach settle down and my heart return to its proper place in my chest before I went in. I leaned over with my elbows on my knees, and propped my face in my hands, examining the linoleum—diamonds and squares marching down the hall.

I knew it was the Birdman on the other side of the wall, but it wasn't him that I kept seeing in my head. It was Mom. And for that reason I couldn't move an inch. So I sat there, staring at the floor until Dad sat down beside me.

"You all right?" he asked.

I nodded, but I didn't look at him. I couldn't. I didn't want him to see how scared I was. So we just sat there, me and Dad. It had been a while since either of us had been inside a hospital. He seemed uncomfortable, too, and I watched him tap his feet against the linoleum. *Tap-tap-tap. Tap-tap-tap. Tap-tap-tap.* Just like my heartbeat.

Eventually, he patted my knee and stood up.

"You don't have to come in, Talia," Dad said gently. "He'll understand."

"I'll be there in a minute," I said. And I meant it.

Dad nodded, and without another word, knocked softly on the Birdman's door. He was welcomed by a warm "c'mon in" from the other side.

Dad disappeared, but I stayed out in the hall, pulling the fractured bits of myself together.

It wasn't that I hated hospitals. I knew that lots of good things happened in them, too. People got better, babies were born—good things. This was a place of *healing*.

It wasn't even that I was afraid of what the Birdman might look like. Even if it was horrible, I'd heard his voice. He'd welcomed my dad just as he always did. And he sounded the same as he always had, bear mauling or not. He'd be out of the hospital soon.

So what was I afraid of?

I leaned back in my chair. Mom's words washed over me.

I guess when it came right down to it, I was terrified by how uncontrollable things could be, and of how terribly small I was, right in the middle of them.

I had no way to steady my heart against cancer, or shifting ice floes, or bear attacks. I wasn't big enough or brave enough to never be hurt, or broken.

It didn't matter how tightly I clutched my fingers around whatever liferope I could find. There was just no way I'd be able to save myself, or the people I loved best, from getting shaken up and tossed around by things we had no power to change, or predict.

But I wanted to try. I wanted to be there for the people I loved. So I took a deep breath and laid my hand on the doorknob. I could do this.

I don't know how long I stood there, listening to the voices on the other side. I kept trying to turn that doorknob. I kept trying to make my feet move, and make my heart quit racing.

But somewhere between loving the people on the other side of that hospital door, and desperately needing to keep my heart from breaking into any more pieces, I couldn't do it. I couldn't go in. I just wasn't big enough.

I turned around slowly and followed the diamonds and

squares of linoleum back down the hall, one foot in each square. And then I was skipping squares. Faster and faster. Until I was running. Past the nurses' station, past the waiting room and the front desk, straight through the double doors and into the arctic sunshine. And I didn't stop.

I ran back toward the blue house on the edge of town, and past it, down the road that ran along the water until I could go no farther.

Standing at the very edge of Hudson Bay, I made another wish and wrote it on a tiny slip of paper in my mind.

I wish I could fly.

Waves lapped over the toes of my shoes and I fixed my eyes on that point of the horizon where the water meets the sky.

As I stood there alone, I let myself wonder, *How far would I have to go to get away from the things that scared me?*

A Good Friend

THE BIRDMAN WAS IN THE hospital for three weeks. He had two broken ribs, a broken collarbone, puncture wounds to the chest, a collapsed lung, and forty-five stitches just above his right ear.

Simon took the bear attack hard, maybe even harder than the Birdman himself. I understood why, though—everything had been just fine until suddenly it wasn't, and it's scary to think of how quickly things can change.

Sura and Dad insisted Simon stay with us while the Birdman was in the hospital. And on the outside, I was glad. But secretly I was afraid to see him. I had been a horrible friend. I hadn't been able to make myself go into that hospital room. Instead, I'd run away.

Simon had been there for me right from the very beginning, when I had almost nothing but my loneliness to keep me company. I was sad, but he had stayed anyway. He'd done everything he could to try to make me feel better.

When he climbed up the porch steps the following afternoon, I wanted to be there for him, but I didn't really know what to do. So when he hugged me tight, I just hugged him back.

"Are you okay?" I asked tentatively.

He nodded, but an unfamiliar frown creased his forehead.

"I'm all right," he said. "Or I will be as soon as he gets out of the hospital."

Simon seemed different. Older maybe. Like the weight of what that bear had done had stacked a few extra years on top of Simon's fourteen.

Simon slept on the couch in the front room, his small brown duffel bag on the floor in the corner, and his guitar propped against it. Seeing it gathering dust in the corner bothered me almost as much as my missing unicorn whales.

I didn't know what to do with this version of my friend. The boy with the songs and stories, with the quick, easy smile, the way he could hug the breath right out of me, or how I would catch him staring at me sometimes—*that* boy I knew what to do with. I knew how to be his friend. It was as easy as breathing.

Being around this version of Simon was much harder,

and I felt myself wanting to run away at times. I was afraid of his sadness, his strange new quietness. I was afraid it would change him forever, slowly turn him into someone else—the way it had done to me—until I couldn't recognize him at all.

One afternoon, a few days later, Dad was at the CSNC, and Sura, Simon, and I were having lunch. Simon was particularly quiet and I couldn't stand it anymore. As soon as I finished eating, I got up and left him to finish alone. I didn't even answer him when he looked up from his half-eaten sandwich, startled by my abruptness, and asked me where I was going.

Sura found me later, curled on my bed upstairs, trying to read a book.

"Can I come in?" she asked, knocking on my door and opening it a crack.

I closed my book and nodded, nervous.

"Did you and Simon have an argument?" Her voice was quiet, and she studied the lyrics to "Baby Blue" pinned on my corkboard, written out in Simon's slanted handwriting.

"No," I said, surprised. "Did he say we did?"

Sura shook her head. "He didn't say anything. You just seem a little at odds with each other."

I shrugged. "He's just kind of hard to be around lately."

She nodded and sat down on the end of my bed, wrapping her sweater around her.

"Yes. Well, sad people can be a bit hard to be around

at times." She ran her hand over the stitching on the quilt across my bed.

I knew Sura was right. I drew my knees up to my chest. "I'm hard to be around, too, sometimes," I said. We both knew it wasn't a question. It was true.

"People are usually sad for a reason, Tal. But you don't have to be sad, too, in order to care for them. You don't even have to completely understand."

I watched her long brown fingers trace patterns on my quilt. "In fact, when you do care about someone," she continued, "it doesn't matter if you understand or not. Loving someone means that sometimes you have to risk getting messy. It's not always very fun, but it's always better than being alone, or watching someone you love hurt alone."

Suddenly I wasn't sure if she was talking about Simon, or me.

"Simon doesn't need you to be *happy* for him, he just needs you to be *there* for him. Does that make sense?"

"I think so," I said, trying to process what she was saying—about Simon, and about me. Sura smiled and patted my knee before getting up and going back downstairs, closing my door behind her.

I sat on my bed for a while after that, thinking about what to do. Try to be a better friend, for sure. But I'd known that when I left Simon at the table.

What I really needed to do was tell him I was sorry.

Sorry for being selfish and for thinking there was no one else in the world with feelings as messy as mine. Sorry for believing I was the only person who understood what it felt like to be sad or upset about things. Sorry for not choosing to be brave.

Simon was a good friend. And now it was my turn to be there for him.

I found Simon out on the front porch, leaning against the rail and staring out at the bay.

"Hey," I said, leaning beside him.

"Hey."

"I'm sorry."

Simon frowned, confused. "For—?"

"For being a lousy friend."

"You're not a—" he started to protest, but I cut him off.

"Just stop talking for a second, okay?"

He grinned, folding his arms across his chest, and waited for me to continue.

"I'm sorry I didn't come to see your grandfather or you when Dad and I got back."

Simon shrugged. "It's not a big deal, Tal."

But I shook my head. "No. It *is* a big deal. You've really been there for me. All summer you've been there and I should have done the same thing. But instead I ran away."

Simon's eyes widened. "You ran away?"

I nodded. "I did come to the hospital. I came and sat in the hall, just outside the door. But I couldn't go in. I—I was *scared*, I guess. And it was selfish. I'm really sorry."

"It's okay," Simon said. "Some people have a hard time with hospitals."

But I shook my head, knowing he didn't quite understand. I was going to have to explain about Mom.

"It isn't the hospital, exactly," I said. "I have *lots* of experience with hospitals. That's part of the problem. My mom died of cancer last year, and Dad and I practically lived at the hospital while she was sick."

Without looking at him I took a deep breath and continued in a rush. "I just kept thinking about her—losing her— and I couldn't go in because I didn't want to see one more bad thing happen to someone I care about. I hate watching pain mess everything up—break everything." I glanced up.

He didn't look at me and he didn't say anything right away. Maybe I'd said too much.

"I know about your mom, Tal," he said quietly. "I've known since that day we visited Miss Piggy. Sura told me. I'm really sorry she died, Talia."

I could have been upset with Sura for telling him, but I wasn't. Not even a little. It was freeing, like a secret I didn't have to keep anymore.

"Thanks," I said quietly. "So, you're not mad at me? For running away?"

He shook his head and stuffed his hands into his pockets and studied the tip of his shoe. "It's hard to know what I'm feeling exactly, but I'm not mad at you. I'm just . . ."

"Sad," I finished for him.

He nodded. "Yeah. And sort of scared, too, I guess."

I understood exactly.

"It's okay, you know," I said. "To feel that way. It just means you love your grandfather. I think there'd probably be something wrong with you if you weren't feeling kind of shook up about everything."

"Yeah, I guess you're right."

"Also," I said, reaching out and taking his hand. "You don't have to be shaken up by yourself."

"I don't?" he asked, holding my hand, tight.

"No."

My stomach was jumping around like I'd swallowed a hummingbird.

"Good," he said. "Because everything is a little better when you're around."

And for a minute, I was pretty sure I could fly.

Rising

WHEN THE BIRDMAN WAS FINALLY released from the hospital, he and Simon moved back into the house they'd rented for the summer. The Birdman would spend the final weeks of his summer in Churchill just resting on his front porch. For a little while at least, he'd have to let the birds come to him.

He hadn't said very much about the bear attack—I think he knew it made me nervous, and when he did talk about it, he tried to make light of what had happened.

"Darn bear tried to give me a haircut and got carried away," I'd overheard him joke to my dad.

But he never really fooled any of us. We knew the attack could have been much worse, and had it not been for that team of road workers, the Birdman's bird list might have been permanently unfinished.

One afternoon while Simon was out running errands, I sat alone with the Birdman on his porch. It was the first time we'd really had a chance to talk since he was released from the hospital.

I made lemonade for us, and as I settled down into a chair beside the Birdman, I handed him a glass. He smiled, sipping appreciatively.

Curling up in my chair, my legs tucked under me, I leaned back and gazed out at the blue water of Hudson Bay, trying to take it all in. Dad and I would be leaving soon, and I didn't want to forget any of this.

"So tell me, Talia," the Birdman said, turning to me. "Have you found what you've been looking for, since coming to Churchill?"

His question caught me off guard because until that point I hadn't really thought of myself as searching for anything, just waiting. I didn't say anything at first—I just thought about his question. Then suddenly, I needed to ask one of my own.

"Do you believe in making wishes?"

The Birdman stared out at the bay before answering.

"I believe in hope," he said at last.

That wasn't exactly what I wanted to hear. Hope wasn't a very dependable thing. It had disappointed me on more than one occasion. Wishes were nicer because I could wrap my hands around them. I could write them on tiny slips of paper and keep them in a jar. I could *control* wishes.

The Birdman knew nothing about my jar, of course. No one did. And it didn't matter that he didn't believe in wishes. Out of habit, I wrote a wish across a slip of paper in my mind, not caring that I was breaking rule number two again.

I wish the Birdman a fast recovery.

My jar of wishes was still lying in the bottom of my duffel bag at the back of my closet, but maybe I would pull it out when I got back to the blue house and drop this new wish inside.

As I sat there, I glanced at the stitches that ran over the Birdman's ear before they disappeared into his hair. They were healing, though that scar would never go away completely. He followed my gaze and gently ran his hand over the stitched-up place.

"We all carry scars," he said. "Some of them are just a bit more visible than others."

I fidgeted in my chair, running my finger around the lip of my lemonade glass.

"But, Tal," the Birdman continued, "it doesn't matter how much time passes, or how many wishes I make. I'm not going to be able to change the fact that a polar bear tried to eat me for breakfast." He was trying to soften his words, trying to be funny, but I knew exactly what he was getting at. He leaned back in his chair, gazing out at the bay again.

After a while he said, "I like to believe that hope, and grace, too, are granting wishes on our behalf all the time. They might not always be the wishes we want, and they might not even be the wishes we've consciously made. Sometimes, we get so busy wishing for something big, we miss all the hundreds and millions of smaller but still-important wishes coming true right under our noses."

I thought about this as I stared out at the bay and spotted a tern hanging suspended over the water. And then it tucked its wings, plummeting toward the dark blue water, pulling up at the very last minute with a tiny fish in its beak.

"See that?" The Birdman pointed.

I nodded and watched in amazement as the little white bird suddenly sprang back into the air and hovered over the water as before.

"Do you think the first time he did that, he knew he'd be able to come back up again?" I asked. "That he wouldn't dive straight in the water and never come out?"

We watched the little white bird as he hovered over Hudson Bay, beating the air with his wings and never seeming to tire.

"I guarantee you he did not," the Birdman said, and he turned to look at me. "But he did it anyway, and quickly discovered he was made to plunge and rise."

"That must have been such a relief," I said, feeling tears begin to sting just behind my eyes.

"I'm sure it was," he said gently. "And do you know what else?"

I shook my head.

"It's only because of his endless plunging and rising that he can fly as far as he does. Without that, he would never be able to make the journey."

Later that evening I left the Birdman sitting on his porch, but what he'd said kept echoing in my brain.

Sometimes I forget that almost everything takes practice. That I wasn't just born knowing how to do stuff, like read, or play the recorder, or go on living, and breathing, and loving stuff without my mom around. Sometimes you have to do things over and over again before you can do them well.

I thought of that fearless bird and the tern feather Sura had given me. If it's true that everyone knows how to fly, and we just forget how it's done, was I strong enough to be like that bird? To plunge and rise again?

The Magic of Churchill

AUGUST SAILED INTO CHURCHILL with warm sunshine and cool evenings. We often bundled up in sweatshirts and blankets, building bonfires on the shore and roasting marshmallows late into the night. I loved sitting out there beside the water, the faces of my friends bright in the light of the fire.

As the Birdman recovered, Simon began playing his guitar again, and he was even teaching me to play. His fingers were so strong and found their places easily, while mine felt clumsy and disconnected every time I tried to press them against the thin strings. I wasn't very good, but Simon was patient.

"It takes practice," he told me, laughing when I got frustrated.

Dad joined us on occasion when he wasn't at the CNSC or with his research team, compiling data. He didn't go out on the water again, but he was still distracted and focused on his work. I knew he wanted things to be different—better—between us, but they weren't. Not really. Not yet.

I wanted to talk, to try to close up that space between us some more—like we'd started to when we were out on the boat together. But Dad was too preoccupied with his reports and looking for his lost pocket calendar.

Since he didn't have time for much else besides work, I thought that if Dad and I could at least talk about the whales, maybe that would help.

One evening, we unrolled maps on Sura's kitchen table and leaned over them, our fingers tracing the whales' routes from previous years as we tried to guess where they'd gone.

"What if there are secret caves underneath the islands?" I asked, resting my chin in my hands. Dad sat beside me, pondering a map of the Baffin Island inlets.

"Hmmm. That's an interesting theory, Tal." He cocked an eyebrow at me and smirked.

"Or, maybe they really are magic," I said, tiptoeing around the edges of my own secret hope. "Isn't that what you said before? Maybe the whales just disappeared into the mist."

Dad looked at me from over the rim of his coffee cup.

"I think I said that *Churchill* was magic," he said, laughing, "and I meant that in a purely figurative sense."

Sura came into the kitchen then, refilling the plate of cookies that sat on the table as she examined our map.

"Churchill *is* magic," she said. She tapped her finger on the tiny dot that placed Churchill fifty-eight degrees, forty-six minutes, and nine seconds north of the equator. "And not just figuratively."

I hoped she was right.

All this time, my jar of wishes still sat heavy and full, untouched and tucked away. I felt them dragging at me, pulling at my heart in a way that wouldn't let me breathe sometimes.

And finally, I knew it was time to take my jar out of the closet.

I sat on the floor in my room for a while, staring at it. I couldn't make any more wishes. The jar already felt too full. The deepest, and some of the most broken, parts of me were written across dozens and dozens of little paper slips. Most of them big wishes. But if what the Birdman said was true—that lots of small wishes were coming true all the time, including wishes we didn't even know we were making—then what was the point of keeping my jar a secret?

Why was I so sure that only secret wishes came true? Was it just easier to believe that because I was afraid of what people might think if they knew about all the things I wanted most?

So I chose to be brave. To take a leap of faith. I'd made that same choice when I fought to find the narwhals, and again when I told Simon about Mom. Being brave takes practice, I guess, like flying. So I took a leap again and set my jar on the nightstand beside my bed. Out in the open. Right where people could see.

Like telling Simon my birthday wish, maybe these wishes needed to breathe, too. So I took another leap, and unscrewed the lid, just a little. At this point, I was pretty much willing to do whatever it took. Because each wish in my jar was waiting for a whale I couldn't seem to find.

Three Little Words

THE PACKING HAD BEGUN. We were getting ready to leave Churchill.

It was weird. I never imagined I'd dread leaving. But that's exactly how I felt. Every time I thought about packing up my things and shipping them back to Massachusetts, a knot twisted my insides and gave me that empty, homesick feeling. Everything I'd felt leaving Woods Hole and coming to Churchill had been flipped over the course of the summer. Home is only home when the people you love live there, and now I had more people to care about here in Churchill than I did back in Woods Hole.

It was surprising really, and I wasn't quite sure what to do about it. I had to go back—to school, to the apartment. And Dad had to teach at the institution. But I knew that a part of me would stay here in Churchill with Sura, and with Simon and the Birdman, too, though they were also leaving soon.

In addition to our personal items, there were several boxes worth of notes and materials that would have to be filed and shipped back to the Woods Hole Oceanographic Institution when we left next week. Dad had asked me to come to the CNSC one afternoon to help him organize some of the data and prepare it for the trip home.

I told myself that today would just be about helping. I wouldn't try and talk about things, or hope that Dad would try to close up some of the space that was lingering between us. Besides, it took a lot of concentration just to sort through his papers.

The back room was piled high with Dad's notes, recordings of whale sightings and the lack of them, audio files Dad had kept while out on the ice, and an assortment of other materials about whales and Inuit culture.

I knelt on the floor, flipping through stacks of notebooks, trying to find some kind of reason or rhyme to Dad's organizational system. I was just about to add a notebook to the box of materials I'd already sorted when Dad's little green pocket calendar slipped from between the pages and landed face down on the floor.

Dad had misplaced it a few days ago, and though we'd searched everywhere, we had come up empty-handed. Now here it was, lost in his organized chaos. I picked it up, flipping it over and flattening out the wrinkled pages. But I stopped when I saw my name written in one of the squares, sitting there alongside a bunch of margin notes. I flipped another page and there was my name again. And again. And again. In every square. I stared at the page. May twenty-seventh. My name was written there for the first time and next to my name, a tiny number forty. That was the day Dad had left to go out on the ice.

May 28th. My name, and a tiny thirty-nine.

May 29th. My name, and a tiny thirty-eight.

And it continued. My name and a number in every square. He was counting down.

I thought about the loops on my paper chain strung across my window alcove. One loop for every day. I'd been counting the days until Dad came back. And so had he.

Dad was across the hall buried in stacks of papers, a determined look on his face as he sorted through his work. I cleared my throat, not wanting to startle him, and when he looked at me his face grew quiet and serious.

"What's up?" he asked, brushing his hands off and shifting stacks of papers as he got to his feet.

"I found your calendar," I said, handing it to him.

"Oh, that's great! Good work, Tal!" His face lit up. "I was pretty sure this thing was long gone." He flipped through the pages, reviewing notes he'd made in various squares.

The room went very quiet and I stared at him, confused. I knew he'd missed me. He'd told me that when we were out on the boat—more or less. But he'd still left. He still wanted to be out there looking for his whales more than he wanted to be with me. If he really missed me all that much, why go in the first place? I had to know.

"Why did you leave?" I asked. My voice sounded hard. "I counted the days, too, Dad. I wanted you here. If you really missed me, why didn't you come back sooner? Or, why did you go at all?"

Dad stared down at the little green book in his hands.

"If I've ever regretted anything, Tal, it's that I was away from you and Mom so much." He scrubbed one hand over his face. "If I could go back and change anything, that's what I'd change. I know I missed things. Entire parts of your life, without ever meaning to. And I could find a whole world full of justifiable reasons for being gone. But the point is, I was still gone."

He paused and took a deep breath. "I didn't want to come, Tal," he said. "I didn't want to come back to Churchill. I didn't want to go on this trip."

I folded my arms across my chest.

"Then what are we doing here? Why are we here?"

"Because, Talia. Your Mom insisted I—we—go. Even after we knew she was sick."

"What does that even mean?" I practically shouted.

There was a lump growing in my throat.

"She insisted I go," he continued, "and she was even more insistent that you come, too, that you stay with Sura while I was out on the ice."

"No! Mom never would have made me go with you just so I could stay behind with some stranger and watch you leave me!"

The lump in my chest was rising. Growing. Making it harder to talk. Harder to think.

"I needed you! I've needed you all along! And Mom knew that!"

Dad didn't look at me for a minute, and then when he did, his eyes were all wet.

"You're right," he said, his voice low. "Mom knew you needed me, and on some level, I knew you needed me. But I didn't realize just exactly how much I needed *you*, Talia, until I was out on the ice." Dad's voice broke and he took a deep breath.

I was having trouble breathing around the lump in my throat. I felt my anger leave, getting swallowed up by all my sadness, and I was doing everything I could to hold it back. But Dad was crying and his words were breaking me up from the inside.

"She made me promise, Talia. She made me promise to go on with my work. She made me promise to bring you out here so that you could see for yourself why this place is so magical. And I couldn't break a promise like that, no matter how much I wanted to. So I went. But I swear, Tal, there wasn't a day out there on the ice I wasn't thinking about you. Worrying about you. Afraid I'd come back and find you'd left me, too. In here." He placed his hand over his heart. "And, I don't know." Dad shrugged helplessly. "Maybe I never should have made a promise like that, but I did. And now maybe I'm too late. Maybe I'm thirteen years too late."

I couldn't breathe. Couldn't move. If I did, it was all going to break apart. It was all going to come crashing in, and I was afraid.

Dad set down his pocket calendar and knelt down, wrapping his big hands around my shoulders.

"I can't fix this, Talia. I can't bring her back. I can't go back and say good-bye the way I would have liked, or give you the chance to do so. Life doesn't give you do-overs. It just gives you new chances. And I think this is mine. I want to take it before it's too late. *I love you*, Talia. Do you understand me? I love you more than I love anyone or anything else on earth, and I will be here for you as many days as I get. I promise you, from now on, your name will be on every square."

The tears I'd been holding back broke and started streaming down my face. Tears of disappointment and loneliness, anger, frustration, grief, loss, and even tears of joy spilled out of me. Hot and fast, they fell. They made my shoulders shake and I didn't try to stop them. I didn't bother to wipe them away. I just let them come. Maybe they wouldn't stop or maybe they would. Maybe I'd always be a little sad, some-where inside me. But my dad loved me. More than whales, more than anything.

He loved me.

And he said so. Out loud.

Because of that, I knew things would be okay. I knew that I could choose to be brave, because that's what love does. It puts courage in all your empty places and lets you believe that good things, impossible things, can still happen.

Dad scooped me up and we settled down on the floor together. He cradled me against his chest and we stayed like that, crying together. When our tears finally stopped, we just sat there, not saying anything for a while.

Then suddenly, I knew what I wanted to tell him.

"Hey, Dad?" I asked.

"Hmmm?" His voice was a low rumble somewhere deep in his chest.

"Do you believe in making wishes?"

He was quiet for a minute and then kissed the top of my hair and nodded, and I felt tears slide down my cheeks again, despite being certain I'd cried myself dry.

"Is this about your jar?" he asked.

I looked up at him, surprised.

"Mom told me about your jar, but I've never seen it," he said. "I figured when you wanted me to know about it, you'd tell me." He paused for a minute like he was searching for the right words. "Wishing can be very good," he said, his voice cracking. "But I think we both know, unicorn whale or not, all the wishes in the world won't bring her back."

I said nothing. I didn't have to, because deep down, I knew it was true. I'd known it for a long time. And I'd been so busy waiting, wishing for something I might never find, that I almost missed everything I had found already.

This place had changed me, because Churchill *is* magic. Here in this place I saw for myself that even the most frozen, bitter, iced-over, and broken places on earth can thaw. Even the ones inside me.

Later that night, after Dad and Sura had gone to bed, and after I'd had time to think, I examined my jar of wishes.

As Churchill summer faded toward winter, the sun and moon had started returning to their proper places in the night sky. It was late now, and the moon shone bright outside my window, casting a patch of silver light across my bedroom floor. I sat down in it, and held my jar up to the moon, shaking it gently so the light could get inside.

Then, unscrewing the lid, I opened it, reached inside, and riffled through my wishes until I found the first one, almost yellow, wrinkled, and stained with my tears. I pulled out that no-cancer wish first, just like always, kissed it, and laid it on the floor in the moonlight. Then I plucked the others from my jar one by one, reading them all until my jar was empty and my wishes were spread around me.

I was surprised to find how many of them had already been granted. It was like the Birdman had said—I was so busy wishing for big things that I had missed all the smaller but still important things coming true right under my nose.

I'd wished for a friend. And I had found Simon.

I'd wished for a place that felt like home. And I had the blue house on the edge of Hudson Bay.

When the belugas went missing, I'd wished for whales. And Dad found unicorns.

I'd wished to have a family again. And I had Sura, and Simon, and the Birdman. And for the first time in a long time, I felt like I had my dad, too.

After I read them all, I carefully gathered them up and slipped my wishes back into my jar. All of them except for two.

I wish I knew how to make crème brûlée.

I wish I could grow roses.

Mom's wishes.

These, I smoothed out and pinned to my corkboard beside the arctic tern's white feather.

"Plunge and rise again," I whispered.

Then I took my jar, tucked it under my arm, and crept down the stairs and outside into the night.

I paused, listening. Everything was quiet. Standing there in the moonlight for a minute, I imagined the blue house smiling down on me as it leaned into the wind—leaned toward the bay, like it had been showing me the way all along.

I carried my jar to the edge of Hudson Bay, and on my knees, I emptied the tiny slips of paper out into the water. I let go of my wishes, set them free. Then I stood there a while and watched as my wishes drifted, like dozens and dozens of tiny white whales, out into the Arctic Sea.

Believing

ON AUGUST TWENTY-SEVENTH, Dad and I boarded a small plane, taxied down the runway, and bounced into Canadian skies, bound for Massachusetts.

We'd said good-bye to Simon and the Birdman the week before, waving as their own plane carried them home.

The Birdman had made me promise to keep looking for birds, and Simon had played a song for Dad and me before closing with his customary bow.

"Don't forget me, Talia," Simon had said as he hugged me good-bye.

"Forget you? How could I possibly forget you?" I fingered the broken-guitar-string bracelet he'd made me. "I'll be too busy missing you to have any time left for forgetting," I said, suddenly trying not to cry.

"Good," Simon said with a crooked smile, and he hugged me again.

They'd be back the following summer, as they had summers before, and as I waved good-bye, I was already counting the days.

School would start for me the first week in September, and Dad had to be back at the institution to teach and report on his research. But we told Sura we'd be back for Christmas, because that's what families do.

Sura was going to teach me to make crème brûlée, along with her famous touton and a whole bunch of other things. I wanted to be a part of the magic she made in her kitchen. I wanted to learn to tell people how much I loved them by the things I cooked for them, like she did.

No one knows what happened to the beluga whales that summer, my first summer in Churchill. Various research teams scoured the coast, looking for mass beachings along the shores of Greenland and Canada—places where the whales are known to run themselves aground. But no trace of them was ever found.

Sura once told me that the Inuit have a story about a young woman—Sedna—goddess of the sea. It's said that when the people no longer listen to greater truths, and grow self-seeking, she weeps and mourns, and all the creatures of the sea leave their dwelling places to go and comfort her. And when the people change, realizing the seas are empty because they have chosen small things over great, then Sedna is comforted. And all the creatures of the sea return.

Sure enough, the belugas returned like clockwork the first week in June the following year, and Dad and I were there to welcome them back. I stood on the deck of Dad's boat, a pair of headphones clapped on my ears, and I listened to them sing.

Dad had a few theories about their mysterious absence, several of which ended up in papers published by the institution. I saved them all and pinned them to my corkboard.

But if you were to ask me, I'd tell you that there are two kinds of stories—the kind people make up to help them explain something they can't believe, and the kind people make up to help them believe something they can't explain.

And this, well, this is a believing story.

Acknowledgments

THIS LITTLE BOOK would not be possible without the support and encouragement of many.

To those who read for me when this book was little more than a dream, especially Jodi, thank you. You gave me hope. Katie, thank you for giving me writing hours when there were none. You made it possible for me to both write and be a mom. My thanks to Leif. "Keep writing," you said. "You are closer than you think." You gave me the courage to believe it. Thanks to my agent, Danielle. You took a risk and believed in this story and in me; and to my editor, Liza, you saw the best from the beginning. And to everyone at Philomel/Penguin: Michael Green, David Briggs, Emily Rodriguez, and Lindsey Andrews, you are in the business of making dreams come true—most especially mine, and for that, I cannot thank you enough. Thanks to Michael Goodyear of the CNSC for answering so many questions—you were my eyes and ears in the Arctic when I could not be there myself. And to Matt Farleo, your artistic renderings of Churchill helped ground this story, allowing me to envision it all the more clearly. I owe much to Steve and Josephine Blanich. Years ago, you faithfully took me to weekly bird-club meetings and unknowingly gave me the Birdman. My thanks to my grandfather Jim. Your real-life adventures as a bush pilot gave me a fascination with the Arctic and a healthy respect for bears. And to my parents, you taught me to read and then gave me all the books I could consume. You never doubted I would write my own, even when I was ever-so-tempted to give up. To my sisters, thank you for sharing this life with me and giving me so many beautiful memories, some of which you may find echoed in these pages. And lastly and most importantly, to God who has given me everything. Every plunge. Every rise. *Soli Deo gloria.*